Readers lov
  series by Victoria Sue

Five Minutes Longer

"…there are no right words to describe the story …
it's just freaking amazing!"
                    —Three Books Over the Rainbow

"Ms. Sue used *Five Minutes Longer* to set up a fabulous world that leaves imagination wide open and a place where anything can happen. I am already excited for the forthcoming books."
                    —Alpha Book Club

Who We Truly Are

"It's no secret that I had a book crush on *Five Minutes Longer* and I can wholeheartedly fess up that the crush only intensified. I'm madly in love with Talon and Finn…"
                    —Dirty Books Obsession

"The deepening relationship between Talon and Finn is adorable to watch and the plot was gripping enough to keep me turning the pages."
                    —Sinfully: Gay Romance Book Reviews

By VICTORIA SUE

In Safe Hands

ENHANCED WORLD
Five Minutes Longer
Who We Truly Are
Beneath This Mask
Guarding His Melody
The Strength of His Heart

Published by DREAMSPINNER PRESS
www.dreamspinnerpress.com

Victoria Sue

BENEATH THIS MASK

Published by
DREAMSPINNER PRESS

5032 Capital Circle SW, Suite 2, PMB# 279,
Tallahassee, FL 32305-7886 USA
www.dreamspinnerpress.com

Beneath This Mask

Cover Art

Mass Market ISBN: 978-1-64108-040-8
Trade ISBN: 978-1-64080-127-1, Digital ISBN: 978-1-64080-128-8
Library of Congress Control Number: 2017913584
Mass Market Published June 2019
v. 1.0
Printed in the United States of America

This paper meets the requirements of
ANSI/NISO Z39.48-1992 (Permanence of Paper).

To my Skype coven: C for her generosity,
A for making me laugh, and P for adopting me.
Love you guys.

ENHANCED WORLD SERIES – Characters

H.E.R.O. Team
Enhanced

Talon Valdez. Team leader. Comes from a large politically prominent family including mom, 4 brothers, 1 sister. Ability – can slow and stop anything in the human body which can either simply put someone to sleep or can kill. DNA changes have enabled him to gain the abilities of the other team members.

Gael Peterson. Talon's second in command. Abilities includes writing and speaking any foreign language without being taught. Can change the composition of his skin to make it a barrier resistant to impact damage e.g. from bullets. Younger brother Wyatt. Father dead. Mom left them when he was a young child. Bad facial scarring on the same side as his enhanced mark due to his drunk father trying to burn off his mark.

Vance Connelly. Comes from a large family all in law enforcement. Mom – Connie. Dad and four of five brothers are cops. Brother Daniel is a senior intelligence officer. Ability – strength. Voice recognition.

Sawyer Rollins. No family known. Grown up in foster care. Ability – deconstructs anything metallic to shavings. Can change his body composition to become invisible but can also walk through walls etc.

Eli Stuart. No known family. Grew up in foster care and secure enhanced youth facility. Ability – fire. Can burn anything including people.

Finn (Finlay) Mayer. Only regular team member at the moment and partner of Talon. Dyslexic but never got his condition officially diagnosed or any help with it convinced it would ruin his chances of joining the FBI. Family – mom, dad (committed suicide four years previously) and brother Deke.

Jake Riley. Regular team member. Transferred from the LAPD SWAT team and became a member of the ENu before joining the team. Partner of Gael Peterson.

OTHER ENHANCED CHARACTERS.

Adam Mackenzie. Finn's childhood best friend and got thrown out of his family when he transformed. Lived in foster care and young offender's units. Currently awaiting prosecution for his part in a bank robbery. Ability – can manipulate electricity and open locks.

Nolan Dakota. Comes from a wealthy connected family and believes Enhanced should be running the country. Currently awaiting prosecution for his part in a scheme to kidnap and control enhanced children.

Oliver Martinez. Eight year old child kidnapped by Dakota. Ability – controlling electricity.

Liam Kendrick. Fourteen-year-old. Can see inside most things, including the human body and the earth's crust.

OTHER REGULAR CHARACTERS

Assistant Special Agent In Charge Anthony Gregory. The FBI agent who formed the Enhanced unit and is responsible for recruiting all members.

Drew Fielding. FBI agent working at the Tampa field office and sometimes brought in to help with Finn's physical combat training.

Doctor Natalie Edwards. the doctor for the unit.

Deputy FBI Director Cohen. Gregory's boss and against the idea of the unit forming.

Alan Swann. CEO of Swann Enterprises. Loudmouth and a fellow hostage along with Finn in the bank robbery from the first book. Likes to appear on television criticizing the FBI and specifically the unit.

Judge Benedict Cryer. retired and standing for political office. Active in his criticism of all Enhanced and wants them locking up.

GLOSSARY

H.E.R.O. Human Enhanced Rescue Organization. Name of the SWAT type team set up by the FBI to include initially five enhanced humans and five regular human agents.

ENHANCED. The name given to a group of humans born in the last forty or so years with incredible abilities that regular humans don't have. They are all male, sterile and the incidence is restricted to the US. The Enhanced gain their abilities around adolescence, often experiencing one or two days of flu like symptoms. The only external sign that forms at the same time is a jagged scar under their left eye shaped like a lightning bolt, and often referred to as a MARK. They are usually superior in physical strength and have faster than normal healing abilities. There is no current biological test available to identify if children, usually siblings of enhanced, will undergo the TRANSFORMATION to become enhanced.

ENu. Police Enhanced Unit. A SWAT type team of regular police officers with the power to forcibly sedate and detain any enhanced individuals.

Chapter One

"WELL, WELL. Look what we have here."

Gael didn't so much as raise an eyebrow to acknowledge the mocking tone. He didn't need to look. He knew who it was.

Shit. So much for him trying to face his fears.

"Are they even *allowed* in here?" a second voice said.

"Better let Bernie know. I mean, he's gonna want to know he's got an *infestation* problem in his bar," the third voice crowed.

"Oh, I think we can take care of his rodent problem."

Gael did look up then, straight into the murky green eyes of Sergeant Mac Carmichael, ENu team leader and general all-around douchebag. Gael yawned deliberately, as much to calm his racing heart as for effect. He took the last swallow of his beer, almost giddy with relief that he didn't have to choke down a full glass. An empty glass was an excuse to leave, right? No one was chasing him out.

"Just let me know when you take care of your personality problem as well," Gael drawled and stood to leave.

Carmichael's hands fisted, but Gael had at least a very satisfying three inches on every one of the guys standing in front of him. He took a step toward Carter, and the man stepped backward. Gael dwarfed a lot of regular guys, and the five feet eleven inches of Mac's teammate didn't even merit a thought. In fact, if Gael had found the situation at all amusing, he would have laughed. But as it was, he was struggling to keep his beer still in his stomach and to make sure none of them knew that.

"Hey, Mac," one of the two guys entering the bar called. Carmichael glanced at them and then back to Gael.

"We still need to have a little talk about your new partner. No one interferes with my team," he added threateningly, then turned sharply to greet his friends.

Gael threw a twenty on the table and walked out. Slow. Unhurried. Like he had all the time in the world. Not like he wanted to run. His *new* partner? Carmichael could have Jake Riley back anytime he said the word.

Gael cleared the door at the same time as a mob of drunken twentysomethings fell out of the bar entrance opposite him, and Gael—heart about to pound out of his chest—ducked his head and slipped into an alley.

Breathe.

It was dark. No way they could see his face, his scar. Making all six feet four inches of him invisible was downright near impossible, but he would try.

They all stumbled past, and Gael had a second to wonder what the hell he had been thinking, coming out in the first place, when every hair on the back of his neck rose, and one hand went for his gun as he turned sharply.

"Whoa."

Gael stared at the man—*boy?*—standing stupidly with his hands raised in a surrender gesture.

"Settle down there, hotshot," the man said, grinning. He lowered his hands slowly without being asked, seeming completely unfazed by Gael's hand on his Glock, by his scar, or by his mark. Gael relaxed his arms and gazed at the pint-sized guy. He wasn't a child, Gael realized now that he could see him properly, but he had to be a good five years younger than Gael's own twenty-eight. Gael's eyes roamed over the spiky blue hair and laughing blue-gray eyes. He had more freckles on his nose than Vance's niece had on her entire face. The fact that the guy barely had any clothes on made Gael wonder if he was going clubbing, though it wasn't even eight o'clock.

The guy took a step closer, and Gael resisted backing up. He had to be, what, five feet four, if that? And there was definitely nowhere to hide a weapon in those tiny black shorts—so tight he would be lucky to be able to bend down—or the ripped neon green T-shirt that strategically displayed both nipple piercings.

"You okay?"

Everything in Gael wanted to suddenly scream *no* until he saw the man was looking at him with concern, worry, and something else Gael wasn't sure about. He took another breath, forcing air into his lungs. He hadn't had a reaction like that in a long time, but then, it was the first time he had gone drinking in a public place on his own in what seemed ages. Make that *never*.

"Maybe we can get a drink?" the guy interrupted Gael's thoughts with a purr, and a bright purple painted nail lightly scored Gael's chest.

Gael finally processed the other look on the guy's face, and his mouth fell open slightly. "Wait, what? You're *propositioning* me?" The question came out on a squeak, and the guy smiled wide and then arched an eyebrow that definitely had been plucked and tweezed at some point. Gael was dumbstruck. The mark of the enhanced was usually enough to send regular humans running for the hills, but couple that with the ugly way the left side of his face puckered and twisted from the burn injury, and most people didn't hang around for a second glance. And this guy… *was smiling*?

Gael narrowed his eyes. He must be high, drunk, and *blind*. Talon had been propositioned before, but not Gael. One evening when they'd both had way too much of the Dutch vodka Talon liked, he had told Gael how he used to regularly hook up. That some guys got off on the danger. Enhanced could and sometimes did lose control, and Gael supposed if that was what one was going for, a mind-blowing orgasm would help hurry things along. The funny thing was that Talon was the most tightly controlled individual Gael had ever met, and of all of them, the least likely to lose it.

"We could go somewhere quiet?"

Gael did take a step back then—not because he was frightened, but because he honestly had absolutely no idea how to respond. "You wanna be careful," Gael cautioned, and the young man smiled.

"Why, you gonna go all Superman on me?"

Gael nearly groaned. The Superman teasing because of Finn was out of control. Gael had hoped in the five months since the unit had been "outed" in the papers, things would have died down, but the press were worse than ever.

"No," Gael said dryly and lifted his T-shirt, clearly showing his gun this time. "Because solicitation is going to get you locked up."

The guy tilted his head in consideration but still didn't look intimidated. "You got a badge to go with that Glock, big guy?"

Gael's eyes narrowed suspiciously, but just as he was about to ask the wannabe rent boy how he knew what Gael's weapon was, his phone rang with the team's alert notification. Sighing, he pulled his cell out of his pocket at the same time as the man took a step back, blew Gael a cheeky kiss, and pivoted to walk quickly around the corner. Gael's phone rang again, vibrating angrily in his hand, and he glanced at the screen. It was Talon.

"WE'RE TRYING to keep it out of the press, but as of today, not only do we have a serial murderer on our hands, but so far the only common thread, apart from the photographs found with the bodies, is that every victim was enhanced."

Great, Gael thought. *Another psycho out to get them.* He looked around the field office conference room. All of the team had been called in to listen to Agent Carl Simpson, from the Behavioral Analysis Unit, who had flown in to talk to them but was leaving in a couple of hours. Agent Gregory—their boss—was here, and a detective who was running the murder investigation. Alik Cortes.

"I can narrow your suspect pool," Sawyer piped up. "Every fucker with an ENu badge, for starters."

The room went quiet. Gael didn't dare look at the guy sitting beside him—Jake Riley, his new partner and a recent recruit actually *from* the ENu—who had stiffened at Sawyer's outburst. Not that Gael blamed Sawyer. Sawyer was the one sporting the black eye that day, courtesy of Gerry Atkinson, Carmichael's right-hand man and the particular ENu *fucker* Sawyer meant.

The enhanced had joined the ranks of minority groups that some cops automatically stopped and frisked. Atkinson had known who Sawyer was but had taken great delight in insisting he was searched. Sawyer had objected, and there had been a "scuffle," as Atkinson had reported it. Sawyer had actually been pinned down by two of them while Atkinson threw a punch. It was wrong, but Sawyer had been late and was subsequently speeding. Talon was furious with Sawyer for letting them wind him up, and then he had put in a complaint against the cops.

"Let me know when you have any actual evidence to back that up, and I'll get right on it," Agent Simpson drawled, and Sawyer shut up.

"So, we have a new victim?" Talon asked.

Gael's eyes rose at the obvious attempt to smooth things over, and the businesslike manner in which Talon brought everyone's focus back to the murders. He was right. Now was not the time for complaining at injustices. People were dead, and whether they had a scar on their face or not, they still deserved all the teams' attention. He glanced at Finn's wide-eyed stare and saw

Talon's hand surreptitiously slide under the table. Comfort. He was ashamed to realize he was jealous. Not that he was interested in Finn. Gael swiped a hand over his tired eyes and focused on the detective.

"Yes," Detective Alik Cortes said, the regret clear in his tone. "Adero Huras, twenty-five. Only family is a younger brother. He worked for a huge lawn-care company his brother owns that has major community contracts all over the Bayshore area. Shared an apartment with his brother and his brother's girlfriend, north of Florida Avenue. Cops have already been there, and the techs have processed the scene."

"What was his ability?" Talon asked.

Detective Cortes grimaced. "I'll repeat what I was told, but to be honest, I'm not completely sure I understand it. Apparently his one love in life was swimming. Like, every day." Cortes looked uncomfortable, and Agent Simpson took up the story.

"When Adero was younger, he won a few swimming competitions. He was approached by a trainer, and there was even talk of possible Olympics. Then he transformed."

And his dreams died, thought Gael. No one said it, but the room was heavy with the unspoken words.

"Anyway, the swimming continued after, but with quite a significant twist. His brother, Mateo Huras, told us that Adero had to go and swim every day or it made him sick—shortness of breath, weakness—and this had gone on since the day he got the mark. But it was what Mateo told us when pressed that was remarkable. Adero seems to have been able to hold his breath for a ridiculous amount of time in the water. He told us he timed him at nearly forty minutes."

"Did he drown, then?" Sawyer asked, confused.

"He was found in bed. No obvious cause of death, no signs of struggle."

"Secondary drowning, then," Finn piped up.

"What's that?" Gael asked before anyone else could.

"It's a small amount of water getting into the lungs that causes swelling sometimes hours after the victim—usually a child—gets out of the water," Finn replied immediately, and Gael saw the indulgent smile Talon sent him. "It causes swelling, which prevents oxygen from getting to the brain. It's rare but often missed because you don't expect someone to drown hours after they get out of the water."

"Which the postmortem will tell us later today," Detective Cortes added.

"And the link is?" Gregory asked. He had been silent up to now.

Agent Simpson opened a file and passed everyone a photo of a young man. Pale blue eyes, elfin, delicate features, and shockingly white hair. "We found another photograph. This—"

"Must be the Tampa Bay victim."

Gael started as the deep voice seemed to rumble from Jake. He took a short breath in and risked a look at his partner. Jake's jet-black hair was cut short, cropped almost military-style, and his steely-gray eyes were fixed on Simpson, waiting for a confirmation of his guess. At least the black eye he'd been sporting a couple of weeks ago had gone. He'd probably pissed someone else off. All the ENu were cocky bastards, and Gael had no reason to believe Jake wasn't exactly the same.

"Possibly," Agent Simpson agreed. "It would fit, except it's a bit of a leap at the moment because we still have no identification. No reported missing

persons, but we would like your team to take the photograph to Adero's brother and see if he recognizes it."

The Tampa Bay case had been ongoing for some
weeks, stalled because they still hadn't identified the
victim. They'd asked—but were still waiting—for facial reconstruction. Gael knew Talon had provided Jake
with all their case files when he started so he could try
and catch up quickly. Their unit would never be asked to
investigate a murder—none of them had either the skills
or the experience to do so. But the victims all being enhanced made them "consultants," for want of a better
word, to the detectives investigating.

"He didn't see it already?" Jake frowned and
looked at the sheet of paper they had been given. "It
says he called 911."

"It was under Adero's body," Agent Simpson said
solemnly. "We are waiting for the postmortem, but unless Adero was the actual perpetrator of the first two
murders, which is obviously a consideration, the photograph is very suspicious. It looked staged." Simpson
looked at Talon. "Agent Valdez, what we need your
team to do is investigate Adero's ability and speak to
friends and his brother. They are very distrustful because Adero was bullied as a child, and we hope you
might have better luck."

Because we share a scar with the victim, Gael
thought, which was why they were all sitting here
listening to the BAU guy. To be fair, Agent Simpson
had been courteous and accommodating. He seemed
genuinely interested in their team and had asked a
ton of questions of him and Talon before the brief-
ing. Simpson had seemed genuinely apologetic that
his knowledge of the enhanced was limited, and with

certain exceptions, they had brought him up to speed as quickly as possible.

"The details we have are brief," Simpson went on. "His only ability that we are aware of is being able to hold his breath."

"But that's not necessarily an ability," Finn said. "There was a regular human from Spain last year who held his breath for twenty-four minutes."

"I don't doubt it," Agent Simpson replied, "but where this is unusual is that Adero could only hold his breath for that length of time *while he was underwater*. Out of the water, he could manage maybe thirty, forty seconds like the rest of us."

"You mean, he could *breathe* under water?" Gael asked.

"No," Detective Cortes said. "Adero's family insists he always told them he held his breath."

"Can we see the Tampa Bay crime scene?" Jake asked in a clipped voice.

It had been six weeks since their partnership had been announced, and so far Gael had managed to avoid Jake, but only because Gregory and Talon had been concentrating on bringing the team's training up to spec. Gael had gone on a ten-day hostage rescue and negotiation course just after Jake had joined them, and after that, Jake had disappeared for a five-day weapons training update that Gael hadn't cared enough about to ask for specifics; and then, as if he wasn't interested in the team, Jake had taken "personal time" for two days, which suited Gael just fine. As far as he was concerned, Jake Riley could take personal time away from him for the rest of his life. He had no idea what Gregory had been thinking, partnering them. Maybe somehow Gael had done something to piss Gregory off.

"Of course," Agent Simpson agreed immediately. "But the site has been released, as we have had pressure from the developers. Having said that, we are very much aware that we need your team's help on this and don't expect you to go in blind."

"Press?" Gregory asked.

"Certainly not until we have the results of the PM. While damning, we don't even have confirmation that Adero was a victim. The postmortem results won't be in until tomorrow, but I'm in court in the morning to give evidence on another case. So while Cortes will be running the investigation, I wanted the chance to meet your team, and I'm grateful you all gave up your evenings on short notice. We'd also like to try to identify the photograph ourselves before giving it to the press."

Talon stood and shook Simpson's hand. Gregory left shortly after with him, and the rest of the team stood to leave.

"What's the plan, Talon?" Vance asked, picking up the photograph of the young man.

"You and Sawyer have your medicals first thing tomorrow. Gael, you and Jake go look at both crime scenes and then see about interviewing witnesses."

Gael sighed silently. Talon had been trying to get them to work together for the last two weeks, and while Gael understood he had to have a partner—hell, he had been the one to push Talon to give Finn a chance—he simply couldn't work with Jake. He needed to talk to Talon.

"Finn and I are going to see if we can attend the postmortem tomorrow," Talon continued. "Eli? How did the weekend go?"

Gael looked up as Eli chuckled—a rare occurrence. Eli was the smallest and quietest of the team. His abusive childhood had made him very distrustful of other people, but their last case had involved finding a young enhanced child in need of specialized care. Bo's ability could be deadly. He burned anything he touched, and in a desperate attempt to save him, Eli had taken the chance that their abilities might be similar and found he could safely touch him. Eli had taken him to the hospital and stayed with him for nearly six weeks while a company had designed and fitted him with a special suit.

"Great. His spidey suit worked well."

Gael smiled. The team had teased Bo because the suit fit him like a second skin and made him look like Spider-Man.

"He's back in the hospital for more tests on his eyesight this week, and then they're hoping he can go to the Landring's permanently."

"Okay," Talon said. "Are you going back to Jacksonville, then?" Eli had been given permission to stay with Bo as much as he was needed until his new foster family could cope.

Eli nodded. "But I'll be back on Monday. Molly Landring's going to come with me on all the appointments this week. She's been fitted with special gloves so she can help Bo get in and out of his suit, and to be honest, he's real happy with her."

Gael scrubbed a hand over his tired eyes and walked to the door.

"Gael?" Talon said. "I need five minutes before you go."

Gael shrugged and sat back down as the rest of the team filed out. He was exhausted, but it would be good to talk to Talon before this went any further. He felt Jake's eyes on him as he walked past but resisted the urge to look up. Finn shut the door behind him, and Gael focused on Talon.

"What's up? I told you my latest tests were clear."

Talon raised an eyebrow. "I don't want to discuss your medical, Gael." He sighed. "How are you and Jake getting on?"

Gael sagged in his seat. "I actually wanted to talk with you about that."

"What do you know about him?" Talon countered, and suddenly Gael was irritated.

"I'd know a lot more if I could see his file."

When Finn had started a few months ago, all the team had seen his file, but only Talon and Gregory knew what was in Jake's.

"You know the decision was made to keep personnel files private to superiors only. Like the rest of the bureau," Talon replied evenly.

Gael nodded. He knew, and he had agreed. But the team was built on trust, and he simply didn't trust Jake.

"So I'm asking, in six weeks what have you found out?"

Gael looked uncomfortable.

"Gael, buddy. What's his favorite color? Drink? Food?"

"I'm working with him, not living with him," Gael snapped, feeling every throb behind his temples. "And don't give me that. We don't all get fringe benefits from having a partner, you know." Talon's smile vanished, and Gael knew he'd gone too far. He put his hand on Talon's arm. "I'm sorry. That was a dick thing to say. I'm just tired."

Talon regarded him steadily. "You're not sleeping."

Gael shrugged. He hadn't told Talon about the latest episode in his fucked-up family saga yet.

Talon blew a deep breath out. "Gael, you have to let go of him being ex-ENu."

Gael swallowed. "I know," he said quietly.

They'd first met Jake a few weeks ago when he was in the Human Enhanced Unit, a special SWAT-type human police force that had the power to sedate and forcibly detain any enhanced considered a threat. All the team disliked them, but Gael had his own personal reasons for hating them even more.

"Jake is decent. He stuck up for us with his team when he didn't have to, and Gregory likes him. We all fought against this, but you know the only way they are going to let this unit exist is if we all get regular human partners. We've wanted this for years, Gael. I don't need to tell you all this." Talon grinned. "They've got Vance's partner picked out, but he's on assignment, so he won't be free for a while yet."

Gael looked at the evil grin on Talon's face. He knew something.

"You look like shit," Talon said.

Gael didn't respond to that. Talon knew the usual demons that kept him awake. He just hadn't shared the latest one. "Talon, you know why partnering me and Jake together is a bad idea." He squinted at his best friend. "Vance likes him. Why can't he have him?"

"Because someone else is earmarked for Vance," Talon repeated, like Gael was slow.

"But he's not here, you said. I don't see why Vance and Jake can't team up now."

"Gael, people are starting to notice. You've gone from the most reasonable guy on the team to the most closed off. You're my voice of reason, buddy.

Always. I've heard more from Eli in the last week than you."

Gael swallowed. "You know why."

"Do I?" Talon shot back. "I know something's going on with you—something you're not telling me. What was the course like?"

Gael tightened his jaw with the effort of holding back the sarcasm. It had been shit. "It was like high school," he admitted.

Talon was silent a minute. "Let me guess: you were supposed to pair up?"

Unreasonable anger surged through Gael. It was pathetic. Like the last kid in the line who's never picked for the team.

"I'm guessing they were surprised?"

Gael had been the first in their unit to get a course. No, that wasn't strictly true, because Finn had taken them, but Finn didn't have a scar. He was more a celebrity than something to be feared. "I had one douchebag who actually asked the instructor if I was safe with a gun."

"Well, that's completely understandable," Talon deadpanned.

And then suddenly Gael was laughing. He was adequate with a weapon, but that was it. Finn was a ton more accurate than he was.

Gael sobered quickly. The explanation of why he had been in a funk was on the tip of his tongue, but talking about it made it real, and he wasn't ready to go there yet.

"I know there's something else," Talon pressed, but Gael sighed and avoided Talon's gaze. "Fair enough, but if things are difficult, that's just the sort of time you need a partner." Gael's nostrils flared and he barely managed to keep his mouth closed.

Talon walked to the door, signaling their talk was over. "I'm going to let you sort this on your own for now, but team evaluations are approaching, and we need this settled before I get the head-shrinkers in here." He paused. "If you really don't think this is gonna work, there might be someone else." Gael looked up hopefully, and Talon stilled with his hand on the door handle. "Let me see what I can sort out, but I want you to go with him to Port Tampa tomorrow."

Gael forced a smile, but he knew Talon wasn't buying it either.

Chapter Two

JOINING THE unit was supposed to be a fresh start.

Jake had been awake most of the night. Did *he* know? Did they *all* know?

Gregory had assured him his history would remain private for the time being. Let him establish himself. Make friends. Learn to work with Gael. Gregory had been so sure they would gel, but even though Talon, Vance, and Finn had been accommodating, Gael had seemed to withdraw more with each passing week.

And it wasn't like he was the first human partner—well, *regular* human; whatever the shit they called them.

Jake yanked open the door of his battered pickup and ignored the protesting whine from the hinges. He had no idea what to do about Gael, and he had no idea where this intense dislike came from. Sure, they all hated the ENu, and possibly some of them with good reason, but the impression he had gotten from Gregory was that Gael was one of the most reasonable of their team. He often acted as Talon's second, and Jake knew they were close. Maybe he needed to fuck Gael to be a good partner. It seemed to have worked for Talon.

Jake groaned aloud, jumped up into his seat and banged the door shut as the throwaway thought rattled around in his brain. Except it wasn't as casual as Jake had been kidding himself. If he was honest, Gael was one of the most beautiful men he had ever seen. The scar on his face didn't make him ugly. It made him seem different, dangerous. Jake wasn't into pretty boys, twinks. Guys so thin and fragile, he'd be frightened to break them. He was a big guy, and other big guys really did it for him.

He shook his head. Gael had to be straight. Seriously, what were the odds?

Jake had watched Talon and Finn for weeks—not in a creepy, stalkerish way—but someone would have to be blind not to know they were *together* together.

He blew out a frustrated breath and started the engine. Why couldn't he have been partnered with Vance? It would have made his job so much easier. In six weeks Jake knew every name in Vance's large family, but he didn't even know where Gael liked to go out for a drink. Would it kill Gael to meet after work in a bar, or even to grab a quick coffee somewhere? Jake liked the Westgate in Ybor. Maybe a little busy on a weekend, and yeah, sometimes guys got hit on as they were leaving if they were into that sort of thing, but it wasn't like every town didn't have its certain corners where one could find someone or *something* to have a good time with.

Jake fingered his cell phone cautiously. He'd gotten the approval from Talon last night to visit both crime scenes, and they needed to start with Port Tampa before the place was demolished. He hadn't heard a thing from Gael, but they were supposed to go together. He dialed before he had a chance to talk himself out of it.

Gael answered with a grunt.

At least he answered the phone. "I'm heading to Kissimmee Street. Do you want to meet first or shall I see you there?" There, he had given him a choice.

There was a pause. "I'm running a little late this morning. Truck's got a flat."

"You want me to swing by and pick you up?" The offer was out before Jake thought twice.

There was another pause. "I'm sure it's out of your way."

"Well, I'm in Ybor, but they have the go-ahead to start construction, and I'm only about twenty minutes away, depending on traffic. We've an hour at most. How close are you?"

Another silence, and Jake's irritation got the better of him.

"Look, Gael, I don't give a crap whether you want to go or not, but the house is part of the site that's earmarked for demolition for the fancy new port area apartments. Cortes got me an hour, but the mayor is pushing this through because officially the site is released, so I'm going now."

"I'm barely a quarter of a mile away" was Gael's careful response. "I'll text you the address." He hung up before Jake could respond, which was just as well. The guy was a jerk.

Jake had to wait a minute for Gael's text to come through and smiled at the irony. They were practically neighbors. He pulled away from the sidewalk.

Less than five minutes later, he was driving down North 21st Street, looking for Eastside Avenue. He nearly missed it, a tiny cul-de-sac before the junction with East Palm Avenue. He just managed to clear a rusted-out car on bricks where the wheels used to be and saw Gael standing on the far corner. He knew it was Gael from his height and build, even though the black hoodie he was wearing was pulled down and it had to be nearly eighty degrees outside already. Then he saw Gael's truck, or what was left of it.

Jake pulled in behind Gael's F-150 and stared. All four tires had been slashed, and there were no intact windows at all. Jake jumped out, immediately feeling bad that he'd given Gael any grief. "What the hell?" he said by way of greeting.

Gael raised his eyes in acknowledgment, and Jake's breath lodged in his throat, words dying before he'd thought of them. So much pain. Bleak, dead eyes. This wasn't only about a truck. Jake took a step forward. He wanted to… something, but he didn't know what, and as soon as Jake moved, Gael stepped back and turned away.

Jake stopped alongside the passenger door. The words *Fucking mongral* had been spray-painted across both doors. "Did you call it in?"

"They can't even spell," Gael muttered by way of an answer and headed for Jake's truck.

Jake opened his mouth to sympathize but shut it just as fast, knowing his opinion wouldn't be welcome. He decided to change the subject. "Should take us around twenty minutes," Jake said, getting in the truck, thinking that might be a little optimistic. "We only got a stay of execution for around an hour." He'd said that already, so he shut up.

Gael was silent until they got on the Selman Expressway, and then he sighed quietly and pulled off his hoodie, revealing the uniform vest they all had to wear. Gregory had eased up with them taking them home because he'd rather them be in uniform, and having to stop by the field office before they went anywhere was a hassle. Jake glanced sideways at the movement and had to swallow his sharp inhale. He gripped the steering wheel a little tighter and tried to push the vision of the smooth expanse of skin from his mind.

"What made you guess about the photo?"

Jake had to think a minute. His mind wasn't on work, and he had to drag it back. "Because the BAU is calling it serial, which meant they had to be pretty convinced even without a cause of death. The only link for the other two, apart from them both being enhanced, is a photograph."

Gael grunted noncommittedly. "Why do you want to go to the crime scene? I mean, it's been weeks and they cleared it."

Jake seriously considered lying, but Gael sounded merely curious, not like he was making an issue out of anything. "My dad worked homicide for over twenty years. He had this saying…." Jake grinned wryly. "Actually, he had a shit-ton of sayings, but one of his favorite was 'a different set of eyes never sees the same picture.'"

There was another short silence while they got off Exit 9. "Did you work in homicide, then?" Gael asked.

"No, I was a beat cop for a few years before I joined SWAT." Jake's hands were suddenly clammy on the steering wheel. He opened his mouth to say something, but the words died on his tongue even as the bitter taste lingered.

"Have you ever been down here before?" Gael asked.

Jake took a breath, glad the personal questions were over. The closer they got to the water, the fancier the houses got on the right-hand side. It was a clear division of money, though. To his right the water views were swanky and well-maintained. The small, battered houses on the left would be rubble in the face of the hurricanes Florida produced on a regular basis.

"Only a ride-through when I first came to the area. The unit's sergeant used to make you orientate yourself for the first few days."

"Carmichael?" Gael said sharply.

Jake nodded, and the atmosphere dropped in the car. The rest of the ride was completely silent.

"We have to tell the site security we're here," Jake commented as they pulled up to a collection of temporary buildings and various machinery. They found the foreman nearly immediately and introduced themselves. Jake flashed his badge, and the foreman scanned both IDs warily. His eyes widened a little at Gael, but he just waved them through after handing them hard hats, cautioning them to report back soon and not to leave the site until they had done so.

Jake looked at the houses. All boarded up. Brick fronts. There were about eight still standing, some so dangerous, especially after *Hermine* had ripped through last year, they had been taped off.

"It's the end house," Gael said, and they both stared. Two stories, red brick, and a lean-to sunroom-type thing to the side. There were outside steps on the other side leading up to the second floor, and the first had a huge boarded-up window that looked like a storefront. "It was a tobacco store back in the day," Gael supplied. Jake knew, but he was surprised Gael had bothered to find out.

"And the entrance to the storeroom is behind the stairs inside," Jake confirmed, and walked to the front and started yanking at the boards. The key to the only door had long since been lost. "They're gonna flatten it anyway, right?" he shouted behind him.

Warm hands covered his own, and Jake jumped and took a step back.

"Let me," Gael said woodenly, and Jake could have cursed. Gael had to think he was flinching at him. He was, but not for the reason Gael likely assumed. This really wasn't gonna work. Jake was determined to stay, to do some good, but he was getting nowhere with Gael, and now... what? He *liked* the guy? "Here," Gael said, stepping through the hole in the storefront where he'd ripped the boards away. Jake knew they'd been removed initially and then replaced when the crime scene guys had finished.

He followed Gael through, the sunlight streaming in. They both went toward a door at the back, or half a door. What was left of it, anyway.

"The cellar is down there."

"It's not exactly a cellar, though, is it? I mean, Florida? Do they actually have anything that would flood?"

"More a storeroom," Gael acknowledged. "No windows."

It had been an anonymous phone call. Some kids thinking they were all badass and going somewhere to smoke weed. They had scared themselves to death and phoned the cops. Jake had listened to the 911 call. Small, scared voices. Definitely kids.

Gael put his hand on the door and paused at the marks. He fingered the scratches and the different-colored paint where something had been. "Locks?"

"Bolts," Jake said in disgust. "They were taken away by the local PD when everyone was done, for safety. A ton of fingerprints but nothing on file."

Gael stared at the door and then pushed it open. He had to duck. Jake followed him in, bending as well. It was a small space, probably 8 x 10. Jake pulled the photographs out of the file, and Gael silently held out his hand.

"The mattress was in that corner." Jake nodded to the top end and passed him the scene photos. The mattress was where they had found the man's starved body.

"How long was he here?" Gael asked quietly.

"They think at least a few weeks."

He'd been just a teenager. A baby. Jake had seen some messed-up shit, but this?

Gael suddenly whirled around and was out of the door back into the store before Jake thought about what he'd said. He took one more look around the empty space and then headed out after Gael. He stepped through the storefront they had uncovered and saw Gael with his back to him. For a second he wondered if it had made him sick, but Gael was standing still, breathing quietly. Jake chewed his lip, processing the hunched shoulders, the powerful arms that were currently wrapped around his body, the bent head.

"Hey," Jake said, putting his hand on Gael's back. Gael stiffened slightly but didn't take a step away. "When I was a beat cop, we were called to a house,"

Jake continued conversationally. "Neighbors upstairs were complaining of a god-awful smell and had called the landlord. We went in. The tenant had two kids. He'd shot the kids and turned the gun on himself because he'd caught his wife having an affair. I was due to take the detective's exam the month after, and I canceled and went into SWAT instead." Jake took a breath of clean air, and Gael looked up, fixing his eyes on him. Jake would never forget the smell as they walked in or the sheer defeat it would have taken to push someone to do that, to end the lives of their children. "That's when I knew I could never do that full-time," he added, dropping his hand awkwardly.

"When I first transformed, I lived with my dad, uncle, and my kid brother. We knew to avoid Dad because he drank, and when things weren't going well, it was better to stay out of his way."

Jake stayed completely still. Gael's blue eyes had deepened, and even though they were fixed on his own, he knew Gael wasn't really looking at him.

"We had a cellar. A proper one. Wyatt had done something to piss him off, and there was some lady coming around from his school or something." Gael's brow furrowed. "Dad said I had to get lost, so I headed for the front door, but Wyatt started crying. He didn't want me going anywhere. Dad blew up. Said Wyatt was going to get exactly what he'd asked for, and he locked me in the cellar. Said if Wyatt behaved, he would let me out." Gael swallowed. "Dumb, I guess. I was only in there for just over a day, but it was the longest twenty-four hours of my life, and I can't think what weeks would have been like."

Jake didn't know what to say. Any empty sympathy would be insulting. "I know this great little café down by the water," he started cautiously. "What do you think about grabbing a coffee before we go see Adero's family?"

Jake waited, holding his breath while Gael looked kind of puzzled at him. Then Gael smiled. His skin crinkled and the scar on the left side of his face pulled tight, but Jake didn't care about any of that. He was too busy staring into smoky dark blue eyes and getting lost in them.

Chapter Three

GAEL BLEW on his coffee, more for something
to do than to cool it down. What the hell had possessed
him to tell Jake that? He hadn't even told Talon that
story. But he knew. It was the room, the small en-
closed space, and he remembered it as if it had been
yesterday.

"Get out of my fucking sight."

Gael had headed to the door, more frightened that
his dad would take out his anger on Wyatt than on him.
He was all of eight years old now; what had seemed
to be a huge number at the time. He would have done
anything to protect Wyatt, and had. He'd forgotten the
number of times he'd gotten a beating because he had
stepped between Wyatt and his dad, so being asked to
get out of the way was no big deal.

But then Wyatt had cried and tried to get past
their dad to get to him, and the old man had really

lost it then. He'd dragged Gael over by his arm—Gael would have to hide the bruise at school—and pushed him behind the door before he'd wrapped his brain around what his dad was going to do.

It was dark. Not just turn-the-light-off dark. Not the whispered good nights or the gentle brush of lips that he could still remember. Not the perfume or the comforting arms. This dark was empty, a yawning space ready to swallow him whole. For a heart-stopping second, Gael's pulse drummed so loudly in his ears, he had thought there was someone else there until he realized the whimpers he could hear were coming from his own throat.

He had stayed on the steps for hours. He could hear voices from behind the door. His hearing was sharp, and he had listened, hypervigilant for any cry from his brother now that Gael wasn't there to protect him. He had finally had to pee down the concrete steps, not daring to move, and he was so thirsty. Gael wasn't really sure how long he had been down there, certainly all the next day because he had heard the TV, and then finally his uncle had let him out with a brusque instruction to get a shower.

Wyatt had cried again when Gael had crept back upstairs. He'd promised he would always take care of him years before, one night when Wyatt had crept into his bed and they'd both heard their mother crying and their dad shouting. Heard the heavy slam of the door and hoped with everything in them—until the game had come on TV and they'd both known the wrong parent had left.

Wyatt didn't really remember their mom, and even Gael wasn't sure if the things he remembered were imagined or real.

"You want something else?"

Gael blinked, realizing he had been lost in the dark. He looked at the cup he clutched, nearly cold and took a breath. "Sorry." Sorry for the coffee, sorry for spacing out, sorry he couldn't be the partner he wanted to be. For a second he nearly shared the letter he had gotten three weeks ago, but he wasn't sure he was even ready to admit that hurt to himself yet, never mind to a stranger. And if he was honest, Jake being ENu was merely a blip. If he hadn't received the letter, he would have coped.

He looked over at Jake's empty cup. "Want a refill? I'm gonna get this warmed up."

"Sure, but to go. I'd like to get to Adero's place."

Gael nodded and took both cups to the counter. A lady was turning around as Gael stepped forward, and her eyes widened as she took in Gael's face. He was going to take a step back, used to trying to appear non-threatening, when she tried the same and seemed to get her feet tangled in her hurry. Her cup wobbled dramatically, and Gael lunged to catch it, ignoring the sharp gasp from her and the sting from the hot coffee on his wrist.

"Ma'am," he said gently, respectfully, and she took a breath, hand flying to her heart.

"I'm so sorry. You st-startled me," she stuttered out, Gael trying not to wince as he rubbed his hand on his pants to dry it. "Oh, you poor dear. Look at what my clumsiness has done." She reached to take the cup from Gael, who was too stunned at her reaction to stop her. "You need some water on that," she confided, worriedly, turning to put the cup down.

Gael opened his mouth and closed it completely at a loss.

"Are you okay?" she pressed, and Gael's throat tightened. Just then it was a little too much, especially from a lady around fifty years old with a soft smile and what must be a kind heart. He wasn't used to concern. He was used to fear.

He cleared his throat, suddenly conscious of Jake standing beside him. "I'm fine, thank you, ma'am. Sorry to have startled you."

She beamed and patted his arm. He was so stunned he didn't take much notice of Jake ordering their refills, or of the lady smiling and going to join her friend in the corner. He blinked and followed Jake out of the door.

"You need me to stop anywhere to get you something for that?" Jake nodded to his hand.

Gael shook his head. "No, it's fine, thanks," he said, still stunned at the way his morning was going.

Jake unlocked his truck and hopped in. "Can you check the address?"

Gael opened the file and typed it into his phone. It was going to take them nearly an hour to get to N. Florida Avenue, and West Seneka Ave was just off that. Adero's brother owned a massive lawn-care company, but he was staying with his girlfriend's family while the crime scene was being processed, and they wanted to talk to him first.

Gael shot a sideways look at Jake when he shifted in his seat.

"Can I ask you something?"

Gael stiffened. He didn't want to dissect his reaction any more. "Sure," he said evenly, really trying. It wasn't Jake's fault.

"How come you got burned?"

Gael huffed. "Because I got hot liquid on my hand?" He tried to rein in the sarcasm.

Jake drew a breath. "No, that's not what I mean. I guess I want to know how is it bullets bounce off you, but you can get hurt by a lady and her coffee?"

Fuck. Gael nearly swore. How the hell?

"To explain, I know what Talon and Sawyer can do. I would have to be blind not to know that."

Gael breathed. Jake was right. He'd been there a few weeks ago when they'd had to walk through a brick wall to enter a building where Finn was being held.

"And you wear exactly the same uniform as I do. You weren't wearing special body armor when you shielded the judge at that town hall demo in March, despite what Gregory told the papers."

"Who else knows?" Gael clipped out.

Jake frowned. "How the hell should—" He snapped his mouth closed, and Gael knew instantly he'd gone too far. Jake brought the truck to a screeching halt. Horns blared as cars swerved to avoid them.

"I—" Gael started.

"Fuck you," Jake snarled, turning to him. "I haven't told anyone. All I've done in the last two months is bail you lot out of trouble wherever I could. I've kept every secret I've ever learned. I even got shit about it from Carmichael." He clamped his lips closed, but Gael heard the outrage loud and clear.

He processed the words. "What shit with Carmichael?" Gael had an awful feeling he knew.

"Nothing," Jake snapped, and Gael heaved a sigh.

"When you came into work all beat up, you said your sergeant was tough with your training, but you meant Carmichael, didn't you? Not where you were training."

Gael took Jake's silence as confirmation.

"It doesn't matter," Jake said.

God, he was a selfish idiot who hadn't given a thought to what Jake might have gone through. All he'd thought about was their enemy joining *their* team. He'd never given a thought to certain shitheads counting Jake as another type of enemy. Carmichael and Atkinson would have taken it as a personal insult. Jake was lucky he was still standing.

Then he remembered Jake had taken two personal days off right after his training. He'd bet the black eye was the least of it.

Fuck.

Gael was a complete shit, and this had gone on long enough. He was punishing Jake for something that wasn't his fault. He was better than this.

"Look, I need to tell you some things. I have some stuff going on right now."

Jake nodded but didn't look excited at Gael's sharing.

"Maybe when we've done the interview and finished meeting the team, we can go get a beer or something?"

"I got my medical at three."

"Great," Gael tried to enthuse a little. "We'll see if any of the guys want to get a beer after we're all done. I need to tell them as well."

"LOOK." AMY Nealson pushed a photograph into Gael's hand. "Adero was the best future brother a girl could want. He was gentle, protective. He would do anything for anyone."

Gael gazed at the photo. Adero was on Amy's left, and his brother, Mateo, was on her right. Amy was tiny, and Mateo was a lean five feet ten. Adero, however, was six feet plus and wasn't far off Vance's size. The big man still topped him, though. Gael smiled and handed the picture to Jake.

"Sir, I know you've been through this, but can you tell me again what you know of Adero's ability?"

"We just don't want the papers making out this had to do with his ability. They might stop looking for the guy," Mateo said earnestly, which Gael understood.

Jake got out a notebook while Gael and Mateo talked. Jake had agreed Gael should take the lead because Mateo had been defensive when he had first talked to the cops.

"How old was Adero when he transformed?" Gael gestured to his cheek in case they were in any doubt about what he meant.

"Twelve," Mateo said, raising his arm so Amy could snuggle closer. "There's three years between us. Mom and Dad died in a five-car collision on I-4 eight years ago. It was their money that gave us the start-up for the business, but it was Adero's idea. I always wanted to run my own business, studied for it in college, and Adero was working for a lawn company at the time. The guy used to make him wear oversized headphones when he was sitting on the lawnmower. They didn't actually protect his ears—they just covered his scar so he couldn't frighten any of the customers." Mateo took a breath, and Amy squeezed his arm. "My brother was the softest, kindest man you would ever meet. The only time I ever saw him cry for himself was when our doctor confirmed that all enhanced were sterile."

Gael swallowed quickly. It was like the universe found new ways to flip them off all the time.

"But even then he said he would foster kids. The ones no one wanted. The ones other people threw away," Mateo said, and Amy buried her head in Mateo's shoulder. "Don't get me wrong, Mom and Dad never once treated Adero any different. They were great. They never once made him feel less than anyone else."

Gael took a couple of deep breaths.

"How soon after developing the mark did the swimming underwater start?" Jake asked, and Gael shot him a grateful look.

"The day after. He'd had a cold, a mild flu. Apparently that's quite a common thing when people change?"

Gael nodded. He remembered his own.

"Mom was old-fashioned. She believed in mustard baths." Mateo rolled his eyes. "A teaspoon of mustard paste into the hot water. Anyway, Adero had been in there a while, and my dad went into the bathroom to check that he was okay. First and last time I ever heard my dad swear. Adero was lying fully submerged with his eyes closed. My dad thought he had died."

Amy excused herself and came back with some bottles of water. Gael smiled his thanks.

"When everyone had calmed down, Adero explained he had ducked his head to rinse the shampoo off and had immediately felt so much better that he had stayed under. He said all his symptoms disappeared. He felt calm, peaceful. We guessed he was under the water for around fifteen minutes before my dad found him.

"We thought it was strange, but you didn't take enhanced to any doctors, so nothing happened until he started getting sick the next night and ran a bath around midnight. My mom stayed outside the bathroom for about twenty minutes until he shouted he was okay. It was a nightly occurrence then, until my mom and dad died in the accident and we went to live with our cousin George."

"George who?" Jake asked.

"George Huras. My father's cousin."

"And he stopped Adero from swimming?" Gael asked. That was unusual. Maybe the trauma had caused the change.

"Oh no." Mateo sipped his water. "He just couldn't do it there. No bath. They only had showers."

"What did he do?" Jake asked, sounding enthralled.

Mateo smiled. "He tried it at the public swimming pool. A lifeguard dragged him out and he was taken to the hospital. That wasn't gonna work, so he started swimming. Like, in the sea. He had to be careful there were no lifeguards, though."

"There was no difference between salt water and fresh water?"

Gael glanced admiringly at Jake. He hadn't thought to ask that.

"No. Like I said, he held his breath. He couldn't breathe underwater."

"And he had to do it every day or he got sick," Amy confirmed.

"Yeah. The apartment block got evacuated once for a gas leak. My dad nearly had to carry Adero to the bath when we were let back in."

"Did he have any other enhancements?" Gael asked.

Mateo immediately looked uncomfortable, and Gael would have been willing to bet the cops had never asked that question. Mateo glanced at Jake and back at Gael.

"You can trust him," Gael said deliberately.

"This is gonna sound nuts," Mateo sighed. Gael just arched an eyebrow. Mateo grinned. "Okay, you win. Sometimes he would suddenly tell us that we had to stop doing a lawn service for a customer."

"What, because they owed money or something?" Gael asked.

"No, for no reason. I challenged him once, and he got really upset with me. Said he knew the guy was a bad man, but wouldn't say how."

Gael frowned. "Did he have any psychic abilities?"

"Not that I knew of." Mateo squirmed.

"Look, we have no idea why your brother died or even if it was an accident. Surely you want this answered?"

Mateo glanced at Amy, and she nodded encouragingly. "We usually did straight lawn cutting, nothing fancy, but a few of our customers wanted a full service. Plants, tree trimming, feeding, etcetera—even some landscaping and designing. That was what Adero used to do." Mateo's voice dropped as if someone could hear. "If he ever wanted us to ditch a client, it was because of him spending the morning in their garden."

"He would hear something, see something?" Jake asked.

"No," Mateo said, wincing. "He said their plants weren't happy."

Gael's mouth dropped open. He'd heard some weird shit in the last fifteen years or so, but that was a first.

Mateo put his arms out, his cheeks reddening. "I know, I know. Crazy, huh?" He leaned forward. "But the last customer he insisted we cut was on Bayshore Drive. Huge house. A month after we finished, we got interviewed by the police because they'd found the body of the guy's ex-wife buried under the patio." Mateo shook his head. "I'm serious. Hell, you guys would know more about it than me."

Jake and Gael were silent for a few beats, and then Jake said weakly, "Do you happen to have a record of the addresses you stopped going to?"

Mateo went pale. "I never thought of that."

Jake extended his hand in a consolatory gesture. "Not for one second do I think we have a rash of dead ex-wives buried under patios, but I think a quick check may be in order."

"I can email you the information tomorrow, detective," Amy said. "But it will be a large list. All I can give you are the customers that stopped our service for any reason. Lawn care is often quite a transitory service. People change their minds a lot when a new service starts up with an opening deal. We didn't keep a separate record of the ones that Adero made us withdraw from."

"Or the nonstarters," Mateo added.

"Nonstarters?"

"Adero was with me a few times when we went to see new customers. He would just refuse someone for no reason, and a couple of times, he went on his own, but I don't have a record of those addresses."

The account of Mateo finding his brother was the same as they had been given already by Cortes. Lastly, as they had agreed, Gael showed the photograph found under Adero's body.

Mateo shook his head. "Who is he?"

"We think he may be a missing enhanced child. The picture taken before obviously." Mateo shrugged, but Gael noticed Amy frowning and passed her the photograph for a closer look. "Do you recognize him?"

She shook her head but looked troubled. "I don't think so. The hair color is quite striking. I think it's more that he reminds me of somebody."

Jake stood and passed her a couple of cards. "If you think of anything."

Mateo stood and stretched out his hand. "It's nice meeting the good guys. I mean, all cops are, mostly, but it's time this country recognized the enhanced for the gifts that they are."

Jake smiled, and Gael's belly did a little flip.

It was comfortable driving back to the field office, 100 percent different from their journey this morning. They'd quickly gone to Adero's apartment but it had been as depressing as the house in Port Tampa, so they hadn't stayed long.

Gael's belly rumbled, and Jake smiled. "Vance organized lunch for everyone back at the shop."

Gael grinned. "That means Vance called Betty's diner and got them to deliver."

When they'd parked in the secure lot, they both piled out and headed to the building and the elevator. The ride took less than a minute, and when Jake bent to tie his sneakers, Gael got a very satisfying flash of smooth, tanned skin.

Talon opened his office door as they walked past. "Jake, Gael, can you give me a few minutes before the meeting?" Talon having his own office was a new thing. Gael was sure he did lots of managerial tasks in there, all of them involving Finn, no doubt.

Gael followed Jake in and stopped in surprise. Vance was sitting at the small table, holding a cup of coffee, but it was the other agent in there that gave him pause: Drew Fielding.

Drew stood, smiling, and put his hand out to shake Gael's, and Jake's when they'd been introduced.

"I thought you'd left us for loftier climbs?" Gael teased Drew. "BAU isn't it?"

Drew shrugged. "No openings at the moment, but I interviewed well."

Gael was suddenly amused. Drew was nothing if not confident.

"I wanted to get you four together to clear the air. Gael, I understand you and Jake aren't meshing." Talon shrugged. "It happens. It's no one's fault."

Gael's heart started beating faster. He didn't dare look at Jake.

"Vance, I'm going to partner you with Jake. I had a partner picked out for you, but his assignment is taking longer to wrap up, so we'll put you and Jake together."

Vance brightened and nodded his approval.

Talon looked at Gael. "Gael, Drew is available for now, and he knows a good deal about the unit, so I'm going to partner you two together. Please bring him up to speed as quickly as possible."

No. Gael had been wrong. He opened his mouth to say something, anything, but Talon turned to Jake.

"Is that okay with you?"

"Sure," Jake said woodenly, and Gael finally dared to look. Jake's face was carefully blank. Gael had thrown Jake's humor and kindness in his face, and a shutter had come down. All the times in the last few weeks that he thought Jake didn't care, wasn't interested, or was simply bored, he was just hiding how Gael's lack of trust and indifference bothered him. If hurt had a color, it would be the deep gray of the eyes he was staring into.

Not for the first time, Gael had screwed up. He'd made a huge mistake—one he had no idea how to fix.

Chapter Four

I REALLY shouldn't give a shit. Jake was used to being disappointed. He'd joined the force to get his dad's approval when he'd really wanted to do something completely different, and it hadn't made a damn difference anyway. The whole gay thing really sealed the deal.

He'd been twenty-two, convinced he'd done everything to make his dad proud of him, and had been careful never to give him any reason to think he actually liked girls. Then he'd brought Terry home.

Terry worked for the department. Not a cop, but a data analyst. Coffee-brown hair and eyes to match. Hot, geeky vibe, complete with tweed jacket and wire-rimmed glasses that made Jake's fingers itch to take them off. His mom had been in the kitchen when Jake had brought him in and introduced him shyly. His first clue should have been her wide, alarmed eyes, but he'd explained it away as it was the first time Jake—even at twenty-three—had ever brought someone home. After all, neither his mom nor dad had ever said they didn't approve of gays, and his mom's cousin had just married his husband in New York. They had sent a nice gift.

He couldn't have been more wrong. Not that there had been loud words or even an argument, but recrimination and *disappointment* had been heavy in the lengthy silence around the dinner table. Terry had gotten the message loud and clear, and had gently suggested afterward that for the sake of both their careers, they ought to quit before they got too involved.

Too involved? Had Terry really thought Jake would have taken him home if he hadn't hoped the relationship was going to be long-term? Even permanent? Jake had quit trying at home, and decided as soon as he could, he would put in for the detective's exam and transfer. For a rash moment, he thought about signing up for the military because of his interest in weapons. But then he had the chance to work with a hostage rescue team on a bank job, and he and his partner had been called to investigate the house with the dead kids. Four weeks later he'd been accepted for SWAT training and moved from Oceanside, just north of San Diego, to Los Angeles. He had trained hard. Already accurate with an MP5 and a Glock, he quickly became accepted as a valuable team member. Until the day it had all gone wrong.

Now, twelve months and twenty-five hundred miles later, he had disappointed someone else. And this one hurt. After all these years, he thought he had toughened up, but he was obviously still too soft. His dad had told him that many years ago, and he'd been right.

He'd been ten, eleven maybe? They had a dog, Penny, that had been Jake's shadow for years but had started to get arthritis. The vet said she could be pain-free with medication. He'd come home from school the next day to find out his dad had shot her. His dad had discovered him by the back of the barn where she had been buried, crying for the first time in quite a few years because his dad said men didn't cry. His dad had scoffed at him and called him soft. *"Man up,"* he'd said. He even offered to take him to the pound the next day so he could pick out a new one. Like a new winter coat.

"So, what do we know?"

Talon's voice permeated Jake's thoughts, and he sat up and focused on his team leader. They'd all written up their reports and demolished the sandwiches Vance had organized. Then Jake had to go upstairs for his monthly medical, and it was after four by the time Talon had called them all in. Gael sat on the other end of the table from Talon, so if Jake didn't turn his head, he'd have no reason to have to look at him.

"Gael?"

Jake sighed silently as all the team turned to Gael. It would look weird now if Jake didn't.

Gael recounted their morning, and Jake did his best to stare at the table.

"What about the PM?" Vance asked.

"Secondary drowning but the lungs floated," Finn said immediately.

Sawyer made a face, like—*eww.*

"It's a PM test for drowning," Jake said before Finn could. "If the lungs float in water, the victim was dead before they were submerged. Although he was found in bed, and I'm by no means an expert on secondary drowning, so I'm unsure why they would do it in the first place."

"The bath was full in the apartment, but Adero was dry and dressed when they found him. They wanted to make sure he wasn't drowned and then put in bed," Finn explained. "They sent samples to get a toxicology report."

"Meaning?" Sawyer asked.

"There were no obvious signs of struggle, so the assumption is that, if Adero didn't kill himself, he might have been sedated."

"But you said the lungs floated?" Vance said.

Finn nodded. "He didn't drown, but one theory is he was sedated and fell asleep, therefore preventing him from getting in the water like he needs to do every day. The only reports we have are that he gets sick. But his PM showed all the signs of drowning, except there was no water."

"That's nuts," Vance replied.

Finn smiled. "Yeah, so we're wondering if Adero's ability is the opposite of drowning. His family said if he didn't go in the water, he developed coughing, tiredness, breathlessness. Sometimes to the extent he 'spaced out,' as his brother put it. All these are classic warning signs of dry drowning, especially in children."

Jake interrupted. "Mateo said once his father had to literally put him in the bath. There had been some gas leak, and they had all been standing at a perimeter away from the house while it was checked out. Apparently when they finally got inside, Adero could barely walk."

"I'm wondering if *not* being in the water was the reason Adero drowned. They call it dry drowning, but in Adero's case, it might have literally been that," Finn added.

"Well, toxicology will take at least four weeks, and apart from the results and the possibility of a photograph that may be someone out of a magazine for all we know, we might never find out," Drew put in, sounding condescending. "To be honest I'm surprised the BAU are connecting it."

Jake saw Gael look to the ceiling and clamp his jaw. *Good*, he thought waspishly. He didn't know Drew, but he sounded like an asshole. Gael deserved him.

"Could someone have come in?" Vance asked.

"The family doesn't know. The brother and his girlfriend were out for the evening and assumed Adero had gone to bed when they got home. No sign of forced entry. He wasn't a huge socializer, but we do have some reports of him going into Ybor. Certain gay clubs, but nothing to show he had a boyfriend," Finn answered.

Just then all their phones bleeped with the special alert notification that meant their team had been requested, and Vance dialed the switchboard. Vance's easygoing smile fell, and the team went quiet as they recognized the distress on his face. He told whoever they were talking to that their team would be there as soon as they could.

"We have to go. Some kid is holding a knife on a teacher at City High. Apparently they're locked in one of the computer labs."

"Okay." Talon got to his feet and everyone followed.

"Talon, do you mind if I sit this one out and read up on the BAU notes so far?" Drew asked, his nose already buried in the file.

Talon shot a look at Gael.

"No problem," Gael answered for him, and Talon rolled his eyes.

"What do we know?" Jake hurried to reach Vance as he strode toward the team's truck.

Talon hopped into the driver's seat, Vance at the other side, and everyone else piled in. Jake hadn't meant to sit next to Gael. Gael looked about as happy at it as he was.

Vance turned around. "Thirteen-year-old. Seems to have taken the teacher hostage." He paused. "ENu are already there."

Fucking wonderful. This day just got better and better.

They pulled up to the school parking lot twenty minutes later, just in time to see Tampa PD putting up a barricade as a news van rolled up.

"How the hell do they know already?"

Their truck was waved through by the cops.

"Talon," Finn said, leaning forward to look behind some temporary classrooms.

They stared as Mac Carmichael laughed and clapped Atkinson on the back before they both got in a truck. The truck headed out of the staff parking lot and onto the main road. Jake didn't think they had even seen them.

"Damn," Talon said.

Jake frowned. "Isn't them leaving a good thing?"

Gael glanced at him. "It means we're too late."

Vance peered through the windshield. "But there's no ambulances. ENu aren't allowed to transport if they sedate anyone, are they?"

Jake shook his head. "Definitely not, and I don't see how any ambulance would have time." Then he straightened a little in his seat. "Talon." Jake nodded to where an older man in a suit was hurrying toward their truck. They all got out.

"Michael Ramsay, principal." He put his hand out to Talon. "I'm so sorry, gentleman. There seems to have been a misunderstanding."

"There isn't a teacher being held hostage?" Talon queried.

The man blushed. "No. We have a small group of children with learning challenges. One of the older boys was tormenting one of the kids in there, and as 'payback' for us calling his parents and suspending him, he rang the police to cause trouble."

"And one of the children concerned is enhanced?" Gael asked.

Mr. Ramsay stiffened. "And why should that make a difference?"

"It shouldn't ever," Jake said immediately before any of the others did. "Unfortunately, this unit has to justify tax dollars spent, the same as everything else. We have no wish to upset or offend anyone, only to make sure a child—*any* child—isn't in distress."

Mr. Ramsay smiled slowly. "The child concerned does have a mark, yes. And I know some of you will especially feel a certain affinity, but I just had to practically barricade the school against a military incursion, so I'm not feeling very friendly toward anyone wearing a uniform at the moment. Whatever else, these are *children*."

Jake knew exactly what he meant. Mac and the others had probably wanted to drag all the kids away and lock them up.

Gael took a step forward. "I have to say, we're intrigued."

"Sir?" Sergeant Hernandez from the TPD stepped forward.

Talon smiled. "False alarm. But I'm hoping Mr. Ramsay was just going to give us a tour, if it wouldn't upset anyone?"

Mr. Ramsay's smile grew huge, and the sergeant grinned.

"I'll get everyone to stand down."

Mr. Ramsay stepped up to a door and entered a code. "The children will be getting collected soon, as we close at five." He pulled open the door and waved everyone in. "We don't have classrooms in here, just one big space."

The team walking in caused quite a stir. Two children came running over, both very vocal with their demands for attention, and Sawyer and Finn immediately got dragged away. Vance sauntered over to a little girl in a wheelchair. Gael was motionless, and Jake followed Gael's stare. There was a boy, around ten or eleven maybe, sitting in a chair clutching what looked to be a children's version of an iPad, staring out the window. Gael took a step and looked back inquiringly at Mr. Ramsay.

"That's Derrick. He is the child we mentioned."

"Can I go say hello? I don't want to frighten him."

Mr. Ramsay smiled at Gael. "He has never shown fear about meeting new people." He hesitated. "He just won't respond."

"Autism?" Jake asked quietly, coming to stand behind Gael.

"Fetal alcohol syndrome, but we think he might be on the autism spectrum also. Derrick is reasonably new here. He lived in a secure residential home after his mother gave birth. He was never returned to her, and she was found dead of an overdose when he was three. He's been coming here daily for the past nine weeks, since his other day care place closed down."

Mr. Ramsay followed Gael, and Jake walked on the other side of him. "He has never presented with any ability that we are aware of. He has some hearing loss and is registered partially blind. He makes sounds when he is distressed but doesn't speak, and we don't know whether he can't or simply won't. Communication is the biggest challenge we face. We have been trying sign language but not very successfully. He loves it outside, and that's where he was. The yard is totally secure."

"How did the bullies manage to get in, then?" Jake asked.

Mr. Ramsay sighed. "We have a volunteer program from the main school. The idea is that kids come here to earn credits to participate in social and sport programs. They were here already, and it was only when we heard Derrick cry that we found the boys had taken his tablet and trapped him in the netting we cover the strawberries with." He blew out a breath. "They were poking him with a stick through the netting."

Gael was already kneeling down in front of the boy and smiling, talking quietly. Mr. Ramsay tilted his head and looked at Jake. "Your colleague has some experience?"

Jake smiled. "He's something of a communication expert." He scanned the room, taking in the brightly colored walls, the soft play area, the ball pit, and the piles of mattresses. "How many kids do you have?"

Mr. Ramsay's smile faltered slightly. "We have the room to take up to eight children a day, from five years upward, but half the week has been reduced to five because I've had to let some of our specialist staff go."

"Why?"

"Funding. Our unit is incredibly expensive to run, and most of our kids don't have parents to fight for them. Currently the state is arguing it would be more economical to move the entire unit to Miami, where there is a similar unit with double the space attached to a large pediatric facility. Obviously that would mean none of our current students could travel that distance on a daily basis." Mr. Ramsay nodded toward Gael. "I think Derrick has found a friend."

Gael had sat down next to Derrick, but he didn't seem to be doing anything.

"Why?" Jake asked.

"Because Derrick hasn't turned away. He tends to put his back to people."

"What is he holding?" It was a small green plastic tablet that reminded Jake of his Kindle, except for the color.

"It's similar to a child's version of an iPad. He came with it, holds it constantly, but it doesn't work."

"What do you mean?"

"At least it would work if it had batteries in, but every time we attempt to put them in, Derrick just takes them out. Even though they screw in, he eventually finds something he can undo them with. He just stares at the blank screen. We were worried it was unhealthy, but it's really only like a comfort blanket or a teddy bear."

Talon came and stood by them, and Jake left them both talking and went to sit down by Gael and Derrick. He took in the small differences in the little boy. His eyes were small for his face, and his top lip was narrow and seemed to be a little out of proportion. His nose seemed short and his eyes were unfocused, but as Jake looked, he turned to Gael. Jake watched quietly as Gael tried to draw what looked like a circle on the back of Derrick's hand. He guessed Gael was trying some sort of sign language. The movement was repetitive and gentle. Derrick didn't look at Jake once; all his attention was riveted on Gael.

Jake knew just how he felt.

"I'm using tactile signing," Gael said in acknowledgment of Jake sitting down on the mattress.

"Because he's partially blind as well," Jake answered, understanding. "I didn't know you could do that."

Gael glanced away from Derrick and over at Jake. "It's kind of new."

Jake blinked. "Are you telling me you've just learned it, or are you telling me you just discovered you can?"

The faint flush on Gael's cheek was his answer, and Jake resisted the urge to exclaim *oh shit* or something like that. Based on what he had seen Talon and Sawyer do a few weeks ago, sign language was really nothing, and he hadn't been joking when he had called Gael a communication expert. Finn had filled Jake in on all the things Gael could do with languages, which was good. He just wished Gael trusted him enough to tell him himself.

Gael had stopped the repetitive movement on Derrick's hand while he talked to Jake for a second, and Derrick suddenly made a low, distressed noise, almost a whine in the back of his throat. Gael immediately covered Derrick's hand with his own, and Derrick subsided instantly.

Gael's fingers started again.

"What are you saying?"

"I started with hi, but now I'm spelling my name. What did Mr. Ramsay say about the LeapFrog?"

"Huh?"

Gael smiled. "The tablet. Does games, spelling, math, that sort of thing."

"He says it's dead because Derrick won't let anyone put batteries in."

"Why?" Gael stopped again but kept his hand on Derrick's.

"They don't know. He just takes them out."

Gael shrugged. "I might speak *enhanced*, but Derrick has a lot of other things going on. I wish I could get him to say hi. I don't even know if he understands what I am signing."

Derrick made another guttural noise, and Gael immediately started signing again.

"He seems to like that anyway," Jake said, almost mesmerized by Gael's long fingers. Then he nearly groaned himself and deliberately pushed the thought away before it could form.

"Hi, Derrick," Gael continued, speaking as he drew on the back of Derrick's hand. "My name is Gael."

Nothing. Gael sighed in frustration, and Mr. Ramsay and Talon came over to them.

"We have been trying tactile sign language for weeks and have never managed to get any response. He doesn't usually like complete strangers touching him. We only have certain members of staff he allows to help him eat and go to the bathroom." While they were watching, Derrick lifted his other hand to his face and traced the scar on his cheek.

"He does that frequently as well," Mr. Ramsay added.

"Has he ever met any other enhanced?" Jake asked as a thought occurred to him.

Mr. Ramsay blinked. "Do you know, I don't think he has. He is certainly the only enhanced child here, and we have none at the main school or the residential home he lives at."

Jake fixed his eyes on Gael, willing him to understand what he didn't want to say in front of Mr. Ramsay. "Maybe he needs to know he's not so unusual," Jake said carefully, feeling his way. He knew by Gael going very still he understood immediately what Jake was suggesting. Those blue eyes rested on his, almost pleading. Jake had watched Gael for weeks and knew his bravado only came with putting his uniform on. Knew he hated his scars.

Jake held his breath as Gael looked down at Derrick. His right hand, the one nearest Gael that he had been touching the back of, was still clutching his plastic tablet. His left hand was fingering his scar. Gael took a breath and gently reached over and touched Derrick's left hand. Derrick went still but didn't pull away. Very slowly with barely any pressure, Gael drew Derrick's hand toward his own cheek. Gael clamped his jaw as Derrick's fingers rested on his scar. Derrick made a surprised noise in his throat. Gael dropped his hand slowly and stayed still as Derrick traced Gael's mark. His fingers brushed the scarred skin under it, but Derrick never reacted to it or pulled away. Over and over his finger traced the mark on Gael's face.

Gael relaxed a little and then brought his other hand back to Derrick's. "Hi. My name is Gael," he spoke and signed.

Jake wondered if he was the only one who heard the effort to hide the pain in Gael's voice.

The whir and bleep from the tablet in Derrick's hand made him jump, and as Jake and Mr. Ramsay stared at the small tablet, words flashed across it. "Hi, Gael."

The biggest, heart-stoppingly beautiful smile Jake had ever seen broke over Gael's face.

Mr. Ramsay's mouth fell open. "H-how?" He managed to stutter out what Jake was about to say.

Derrick let his hand fall down and he gripped the small tablet tighter. Just then the doors at the back of the room opened and some ambulance drivers walked in.

"It's Derrick's transport," he said faintly.

Gael immediately signed on the back of Derrick's hand. "I promise I will come and see you as soon as I can," he said out loud at the same time, and then he stood.

Mr. Ramsay seemed to realize he was still standing openmouthed and hurried to organize the children going home.

"EVERYTHING OKAY?" Talon asked as the other guys stepped up to Jake and Gael.

Vance shrugged. He'd been sitting with the little girl in the wheelchair. Jake smiled. In the last few weeks, he had spent the most time with Vance and knew Vance's shrug wasn't because he was unaffected. It would have been the exact opposite.

Jake was quiet as they drove back to the office, still stunned at what he had seen and completely unsure of whether to talk about it.

"Derrick was able to power the tablet himself," Gael said. "He only got a 'Hi, Gael' out, but the machine had no batteries in."

Jake held his breath, and after a few seconds, looked around at the other guys.

Vance grinned. Finn nodded.

"Good for him," Talon said quietly.

Jake took a breath, but he got it. Their abilities were amazing. Jake was sure he didn't know everything they could do. Making a kid's computer screen turn on by itself was merely a blip on their radar.

"How much funding do they need do you think?" Finn asked suddenly.

Jake smiled wryly to himself. He seemed to be the only one sitting in the car who was impressed at all.

"I don't know. Did he mention it to you, Talon?" Gael asked. Talon grinned, and Gael narrowed his eyes. "What are you planning?"

"I have an aunt who's a producer of a TV program called *Double Standards*."

Jake looked at Talon. "I've heard of that." He couldn't for the life of him remember where from, though.

"Oh yes," Vance exclaimed. "My mom loves that show."

"What is it?" Sawyer asked.

"Well, each week they pick a deserving cause and give the family, supporters, whoever seven days to raise as much cash as they can, up to quarter of a million dollars," Vance explained. "Whatever they raise, the program matches—hence *Double Standards*."

"Two hundred and fifty thousand is a great chunk of change, but I would imagine even that won't go far for this place," Jake said.

"But the publicity they get from the program usually doubles, even triples it," Vance said. "Long-term it's a great thing. Talon, you gonna call her?" Vance and Finn immediately started plotting various fundraising ideas.

"You know," Vance said after another minute, "I bet my dad could get the guys down at the precinct in on this. They're always up for a charity football match or something."

Jake let the chatter go on around him. The truck was warm, he was tired, and he was still trying to process what he had seen. He saw Gael rubbing his eyes once or twice and surreptitiously studied him. He had said there was something he wanted to tell him. Gael had mentioned asking everyone out for a drink after work, but to be honest, he looked beat and was struggling to keep his eyes open.

When they got back to the office, Drew was talking to Cortes, and Jake quickly brought them both up to speed with the interview they had done with Mateo Huras. Gael continued explaining everything about Adero's background and, more importantly, mentioned the incident with the dead ex-wife.

"Jesus. That was Miriam Jenner. I worked that case." Cortes was stunned. He glanced at everyone. "You think this has credibility? Seriously? It sounds like something off a bad sci-fi flick."

Gael sighed. "My *life* has been a bad sci-fi flick for eighteen plus years."

Cortes looked stricken. "I'm—"

Gael waved his apology away. "Sorry, I'm a little wiped out."

Cortes excused himself and left, eager to follow up on what he had been told.

"I hear the school was a false alarm?" Gregory said as he came into the room.

Jake jumped in and praised Gael for how he'd clicked with Derrick, and said he had communicated with the boy using a child's computer. He never mentioned the battery issue. Gael's eyes were warm on his, and he struggled not to keep glancing at them.

"They're struggling for funds," Vance said and explained their fundraising idea.

"This is exactly the sort of thing we need for the team," Gregory enthused. "Gael, maybe you and Drew can go back there tomorrow? I'm sure the department will want to get behind this." He rubbed his hands eagerly and beamed at everyone, including Jake.

Jake felt like he'd been kicked. He stepped back a little while Drew chatted with Gael, saying he wished he hadn't been reading case files while all the excitement was happening. Jake stayed quiet. He knew if he opened his mouth, resentment would come flooding out. He wanted to be the one to go back with Gael tomorrow. Childish, pathetic, but....

"Why don't you go home?" Talon interrupted his thoughts, and Jake blinked, but Talon was looking at Gael, not him. "You can write up your report at home and send it in." He looked around. "In fact, you all look beat. Let's call it a day and see what turns up tomorrow."

Everyone stood, and Jake edged closer to Gael. "You might as well get a ride with me. I'm only five minutes away."

Gael looked startled, and Jake was willing to bet he'd never given his damaged truck another thought.

They walked out mostly in silence. It was only a little after five, but Gael looked like he hadn't slept properly. In fact, he looked like shit. If it wasn't for some report Jake had read saying the enhanced didn't get sick, he'd have said Gael was coming down with the flu or something.

They headed for Jake's battered pickup that he'd never gotten around to selling, and Jake opened the door. Gael got in and leaned back, blinking wearily. Jake tuned the radio to the soft jazz he liked, and he was willing to bet it wouldn't take Gael more than a couple of minutes until both his eyes shut.

Jake pulled up as the lights turned red and looked at Gael. Big guy, not huge like Vance, but definitely Talon's size and bigger than Jake's own five feet eleven. Jake worked out and liked to think he was in good shape, but he honestly wouldn't be surprised if Gael could hold him down with one hand. He clamped his lips shut to stop himself groaning out loud and shivered, which was nuts, as it had been heat, not cold, that had rushed through his body. He wrenched his eyes away from Gael just as the light changed.

Fifteen minutes later he pulled up outside Gael's. The truck was still in the sorry state it had been this morning, but somehow he didn't think their friendship was.

Chapter Five

As THE truck came to a stop, Gael jerked awake in a panic. He'd trained himself to sleep lightly, and even though it had been years since his bed had been a few cardboard boxes, it still took nothing to wake him. What shocked him was that he had fallen asleep in the first place.

"Would you like a coffee or a beer or something?" The words were out before he knew he was going to say them. "That's if you don't want to go to bed." *Shit.* "I mean, you might be tired and want to go home." He groaned and thunked his head back on the seat.

A low chuckle had him opening his eyes again. Jake's eyes were… *dancing*, for want of a better word, and Gael grinned.

"Open mouth, insert foot."

It took a second and Jake pulling in a sharp breath before Gael realized his last comment, while not as suggestive as the first, could also make his brain go somewhere else. He gave up and opened the door. He didn't know what to think when Jake cut the engine and opened his own door.

Gael picked his way through the various trash littered on the sidewalk, barely gave the truck a second glance, as he had no idea what to do about it, pulled his door key from his pants pocket, and took the two steps to the door. He cringed at the peeling paint and the general feeling of drabness and quickly keyed in the code to silence the alarm after he had opened the door. Gael flicked on the light and stepped into one of the three rooms in his ground-floor apartment.

He looked around critically, not sure why he wanted Jake to like the space. The two massive recliners suddenly screamed "old man" when they had always meant lazy Sunday afternoons catching a game. The large flat-screen seemed to shout that he had nothing better to do, and the beige-and-chocolate color scheme looked boring.

"Nice," Jake said with what seemed to be genuine admiration in his voice.

Gael waved him to a seat. "Coffee or beer?"

"What you got?"

"Wild Night," Gael said without thinking, then wished for lightning to strike him where he stood when Jake grinned.

"I meant beer, but whatever."

Heat flushed through Gael at rocket speed, and he strode to the refrigerator in case he was likely to spontaneously combust. *Jake is gay?* "It's a local Florida brewery, Swamp Head," he rushed out in explanation. "Midnight Oil, Stump Knocker, Wild Night."

Gael looked up when Jake didn't reply to find him studying his music collection.

"Eric Darius?" He turned over the CD.

"Local to Tampa actually," Gael supplied, grabbing the bottles and an opener. "Saxophonist," he added by way of an explanation.

Jake nodded and put the CD down, then took a bottle from Gael. "I like Mindi Abair. Did you hear her record with Aerosmith?"

Gael smiled in delight. "You like jazz?"

"I like most things to be honest. Not so much heavy metal, and I don't like full orchestra, but people don't have to sing for me to like their music." Jake eased down into one of the leather recliners. "How long have you lived in Ybor?"

"I grew up in Charlottesville and eventually moved to Tampa. Got a job on the docks and met Talon there. I roomed with Talon for a while, and then I got this place." Gael gazed around the room. "It's small, but there's only me." *Shit*, could he sound any more pathetic?

"You have a brother, right?"

A warm feeling spread through Gael. "Yeah, Wyatt. He's just graduated from Georgetown." He couldn't keep the pride out of his voice, but he didn't care.

"You got any other family?" Jake asked.

The temperature suddenly took a drop in the room, and Gael's blood seemed to prick his skin from the inside. Smooth warmth had been replaced with brittle cold. Gael lurched to his feet. "You want another one?"

Jake looked down at his bottle. "No, I'm good," he said slowly.

Gael was grateful Jake didn't point out that he'd barely had time to take more than one swallow from his still mostly full bottle. He moved back to the fridge, not really knowing why, because he hadn't drunk any more than Jake. He turned around to face Jake, to offer some sort of explanation for his shitty mood, but Jake was there behind him. How had he not heard him move?

Jake drew a hand through his thick black hair, and Gael watched as his fingers trailed through it. "Maybe this was a bad idea," he said slowly.

Gael tried to process the words, but his eyes were fixed on the pink lips they were moving through. He swallowed. "Because?"

Jake stared into Gael's eyes. Gael took a breath, then another one as Jake seemed to swallow all his oxygen. "Because," Jake whispered, taking a step closer, his hand sliding around the back of Gael's neck, "I want to do this." He breathed the word out as his lips ghosted over Gael's.

Gael leaned forward, his chilled body seeming to know it needed Jake's heat and seeking it out. Gael ignored the whimper from his own throat and slid his hands up Jake's back, feeling the hardness, the strength. He opened his mouth, and Jake instantly pushed his tongue in, stroking, exploring. Teasing every shudder out of Gael, his arms clutching him tighter to show he liked it. On and on the kiss went, demanding, domineering, until the only thing keeping Gael balanced was the heavy hand threading through his hair as Jake leaned him back. For a second Gael's brain went fuzzy, and he suddenly wrenched his mouth away for oxygen. He had been so lost he hadn't realized he needed it. Jake immediately moved his lips to Gael's throat and gently mouthed the skin. Gael wobbled. He'd always thought *going weak at the knees* was a cheesy line until he actually felt it.

"How about I stay, and then I can give you a ride to work again tomorrow?" Jake panted, as though words were an effort.

But they were the equivalent of a cold shower. Gael stepped back, and it was Jake's turn to stumble. He bit his lip, and Jake searched his gaze until Gael dropped it.

Jake gave a little sigh. "Maybe you're right. We could probably both do with an early night." He took a step back with a slight shake of his head, as if to clear it. "I don't think we have anything going on early tomorrow, so I'll be around at eight thirty unless we get a call or something." He hesitated. "Unless you need help getting your truck anywhere tonight?" He looked at his watch. "What did the insurance guys say?"

Inexplicable temper flared in Gael, and he scoffed. "Insurance?"

Jake looked puzzled. "Yeah. Do you need a police report? Maybe we can ask Vance—"

"You're really clueless, aren't you?" Gael bit out. "Enhanced don't get insurance. I only get mine because I have an approved job."

"Gael, buddy—" Jake sounded apologetic.

"I'm not your buddy," Gael nearly yelled, not wanting to be patronized. "You want to work with us, you should have done your homework. My so-called insurance only covers me for damage to other cars. It's taken out of every pay check automatically as a condition of employment, and I pay $600 a month for a crappy piece of paper that means I will only ever get to live in a dump like this," he roared finally, the volume increasing with every word.

Jake opened his mouth and closed it without saying a word.

"Get out." Gael thought he was going to have something—some*one*—of his own, but this would never work.

"Get out?" Jake parroted in disbelief. Then, with sarcasm dripping from every word, he said, "Wow. You were right when you said I hadn't done my homework. Tell me, where does it say that all enhanced are assholes?"

Gael lunged before he thought better of it, and Jake sidestepped, whirling around and grabbing Gael by his neck. In a second he had his arm around his throat and a hand to the back of his head. Gael held his breath, stunned at how fast Jake had moved. He could snap Gael's neck. Jake blew out a short breath and stepped away, releasing Gael instantly. He didn't even bother with a backward glance as he strode to the door and yanked it open. Gael couldn't help the wince as Jake slammed it shut behind him.

"Fuck," Gael spat out into the silence, sliding down with his back against the wall. What the hell had just happened? Jake was right—when had he become such an asshole?

THE NEXT morning Jake pulled into Gael's street. He'd thought long and hard last night after he had calmed down. He knew something was up with Gael. He knew that. Why had he pushed, and then why had he treated Gael like some one-night stand? Gael was better than that. *Jake* was better than that. He'd gotten exactly what he deserved last night, and Gael might have been an ass, but he was right about one thing: Jake should know more about the people he was working with. Before he'd gone to bed last night, he had hit the internet.

Once he got through the *blah*, *blah* about the early years, he had found some career links. He knew the enhanced weren't allowed passports. The incidence of enhanced transformation was restricted to the US, which was completely fascinating. Not that other countries wanted them, but why would something that seemed like advanced human evolution be restricted to one country? There was a team of scientists at Stanford University doing research on just that. He scrolled past the figures ranking the university first in the country for biological science, chemistry, and physics, and read the call they had posted asking for enhanced volunteers to help them with research. He wondered if the team knew. He would bet Finn did.

None of the information he found last night, while broadening his education certainly, gave him any clues on how to deal with Gael. He had no idea what to do, except possibly grovel. He'd even gone to Starbucks on his way here, hoping the ambrosia of the gods would smooth an apology. Last night was all on him. He'd known something was bothering Gael, and for the first time in a few weeks, he didn't think that something was Jake himself.

He was lost in his head a little as he pulled up outside Gael's apartment and didn't notice anything until he stepped out onto the sidewalk and looked up.

Shit.

He recognized the spray paint immediately, exactly like the truck. And as if that wasn't enough, the same bad spelling, as the word *mongral* had been sprayed all over his front door. As he wondered whether to pull out his cell and call Talon or Vance, the door opened and Gael stepped out with a cardboard box. He didn't even see Jake, and Jake watched the defeated slump of shoulders, the shuffled steps, the downturned mouth, and he felt even worse than he had last night.

"Hey," he called out softly, holding up the coffee cups.

Gael looked up, startled, and his nose flared as he took a couple of hurried breaths. Jake walked up to him, needing to make things right but not wanting a conversation on the street. Gael took an immediate step back inside.

"I owe you an apology," Jake said quietly as soon as he got close enough.

Gael took a breath and stepped farther back inside the house. "Come in, because so do I."

Jake smiled; he couldn't help it. "I was way out of line last night, and it won't happen again." He passed Gael a cup.

Gael tilted his head to one side. The *really* was unspoken but heard loudly. Jake glanced behind Gael at the boxes, the suitcases. Gael followed his look and took a tentative sip of his coffee. A flash of surprise crossed his face when he tasted the caramel. Jake smiled. He tried to take notice of things when he could.

"Landlord called an hour ago. He wants me out by twelve."

"Why?" Jake asked in astonishment. "Can he do that?"

Gael heaved a sigh. "You saw outside? You must have," he said, answering his own question. "The noise woke me up around one, but they'd gone before I got to the door. Anyway, the landlord found out, and I have to leave."

"But," Jake started, "it wasn't your fault."

"He threatened to call the cops," Gael said. He gestured to his mark. "And we both know who would have turned up and loved every second of it."

Jake swallowed more protests down. He didn't want to get chewed out again. "Where are you going?"

Gael hesitated. "Vance has an empty garage at his mom's. They'll store my stuff. I was just gonna call them."

"So you're going to stay there?"

Gael shook his head. "No. Connie has recently started fostering again. She got an emergency placement two days ago, and they're full. Don't get me wrong, I could sleep on the couch, but I don't want to make things awkward for them."

"Vance's dad would give you shit?" Surely not—his son was enhanced.

"Oh, no." Gael shook his head. "Nothing like that. I just know Connie is due an inspection soon or something. There are certain people in their neighborhood causing trouble about her fostering enhanced. Saying they are dangerous and should be locked up. I don't want me sleeping on her couch to give them any ammunition."

"So, where are you going?" Jake asked carefully, and Gael smiled brightly.

"I know a guy who rents rooms. I'll be fine."

Jake wasn't sure who Gael was trying to convince, but it wasn't working. He bent and picked up a box. "Have you called Vance to help you move any of this yet?"

"No. Like I said, I was just going to."

Jake smiled. "Don't bother. You're coming to my place." He strode to his truck before Gael had time to get a word out.

"I can't do that," Gael insisted, following him.

"Why?" Jake asked. "I have a spare bedroom, and I promise not to jump you."

Gael's mouth fell open.

Jake might have admitted to enjoying himself a tiny bit. "We still have to take the big stuff to Vance's, but let's get everything in the truck, and then you can decide."

"I actually need to drop the keys to my truck at Vance's. He's got a cousin who's got a garage he can transport it to. I was an ass last night," he admitted. "I don't want you thinking this is going to spill over at work. Believe it or not, I can be a grown-up."

Jake nodded and went for another box. In less than ten minutes, they had the truck loaded. Apparently the bedroom furniture had been rented with the house, and Gael insisted he didn't want the recliners. They were old. Jake shrugged. He'd thought they were kinda comfy, but whatever.

They pulled up at Vance's less than an hour later, and Gael chuckled and nodded to Talon's beast sitting outside. "I think Vance told his mom we were coming and she asked everyone over for pancakes."

Jake's stomach growled. It had been a long time since his coffee, and he deliberately had left that morning with no breakfast, hoping to persuade Gael to stop for some.

"Have you met Connie?"

Jake shook his head just as a teenager came down the path at the side of the house.

"Gael," he yelled happily, and Gael strode toward him, enveloping him in a big bear hug.

"Hey, Liam, how's school?"

Liam's smile was huge. "Professor Reed from UCF is coming to talk about tectonics."

Gael grinned, and Jake instantly knew who the boy was. Liam, the enhanced child who could literally see beneath the earth's crust. It was completely mind-boggling.

Liam glanced at Jake and smiled happily. He put out his hand. "You're Jake."

Jake shook it solemnly, realizing he had seen Liam briefly at the whole mess with Alan Swann a few weeks ago. He would never have recognized the smiling, happy kid. "Good to meet you properly."

Liam smiled back at Gael. "Gotta run. The bus will be here soon." He ran down the sidewalk and disappeared around the corner.

Gael walked up the path that Liam had come from, and Jake followed him. The kitchen door opened before Gael got a chance to knock on it. An older woman with gray curls and a huge smile threw her arms around Gael, and Gael soaked it up. "I haven't seen you in two weeks," she chided softly before turning her attention to Jake.

He put his hand out. "Nice to meet you, ma'am."

Connie batted his arm away and flung her arms around him as Gael stepped into the kitchen. She released him after a minute and gazed up at him. "Are you Gael's new partner?"

Jake sighed. He wished.

She smiled gently and shooed him forward. "The gang's all here."

Jake walked in and was surprised to see so many people sitting around a huge wooden table. Vance grinned and waved him to the empty seat next to Gael. An older man in uniform looked up as Jake came in. Jake stood smartly, instantly recognizing the single silver bar.

Lieutenant Connelly nodded his acknowledgment and got up, shaking Jake's hand. "I know of your father. Good policeman."

"Thank you, sir," Jake replied respectfully and sat down. Before he had chance to ask any questions, a full breakfast was put down in front of him. He stared in astonishment at the bacon, eggs, and home fries. A huge pile of pancakes was pushed toward him as well. His belly growled noisily, and Gael chuckled.

When they'd all eaten, Connie disappeared with Vance's dad, leaving him and Gael, Talon, Finn, Vance, and Sawyer sipping coffee. Gael put down his cup and took a breath. As if a switch flicked, the team looked at him expectantly.

"I need to tell you guys something."

"About damn time," Talon said, and Jake looked at him sharply, but it made sense. He knew they were best friends.

"I know, and I'm sorry I didn't say anything earlier to any of you."

Jake raised his eyebrows. Maybe Gael hadn't told Talon anything.

"You don't have to tell us jack if you don't want to," Sawyer said.

"You speak for yourself," Vance grumbled. "Should I put another pot on?" he asked seriously. "My mom always used to ask us if this was a one pot or a two'er when we were kids," he offered.

Gael smiled weakly as Vance put two on when the team waved their empty mugs. "You all know that my mom left me, my dad, and Wyatt when I was six?"

Jake looked up in surprise. He certainly hadn't. No one said anything, just listened quietly.

"Thing is, when I got back from that hostage negotiation course, there was a letter waiting for me. It had been passed on through the department." Gael blew out a breath. "It was from my half sister. She lives in Texas."

Jake edged closer. He could practically feel Gael's distress, but he wasn't sure if anything he could say or do would be welcomed.

"I didn't know you had a half sister," Talon said.

Gael shrugged. "Neither did I."

"So, this is your mom's daughter?" Vance clarified.

"Yeah. Long story short, my mom moved back in with her mom. They'd been estranged because of my dad. Dad always said she ran off with someone else, but I don't know for sure. My gran died three months after that, but by that time, my mom was definitely seeing someone else. They got married two years later when she divorced my dad." Gael looked at Talon. "I never knew they'd even divorced, but there were a lot of papers burned when the house went up."

Jake's ears pricked up. There had been a fire?

"My mom remarried and had my sister. She never knew about me until she found some news clippings my mom had in a shoebox. One was the report of us at the press conference. Another was the picture of me and that judge. There was another of the press conference Alan Swann held at Liam's dad's funeral. Anything about the team, she'd kept. Anyway, Louise, my sister, wrote to the department, and they passed it to me."

"Wow," Finn said. "That's amazing. I would love to have a sister."

Talon leaned forward. "But?" Talon voiced exactly what Jake was thinking. There was something else.

"Her husband died seven years ago in a motor-bike accident. My mom had breast cancer and died just six weeks ago."

Oh shit. Hundreds of thoughts ran through Jake's brain, and before he even thought about it, he put a comforting hand on Gael's knee. As soon as he touched Gael's leg, he yanked it away quickly. Gael swallowed, and Talon asked another question.

"Are you going to meet her?"

Jake's heart pounded. He'd promised not to touch Gael, and here he was, doing it anyway.

"I don't know," Gael said after a few seconds and slowly panned to Jake.

Jake froze and got to see a look he wasn't expecting. It hadn't been censure. For a giddy second, he thought about putting his hand back.

"Texas?" Vance queried.

"Usually, yeah, but she and her husband are on vacation this week. Disney," Gael said with a certain helplessness.

"A neutral territory would be good," Finn offered.

"And you know any one of us would go with you if you needed us to," Talon said.

Gael glanced back at Jake just as the alert sounded on their phones.

Sawyer grumbled, got out his cell phone, and dialed the office. He took a breath as he listened and his green eyes widened. "Yes, sir. About thirty minutes." He wordlessly passed Talon the phone. "There's been another murder," he said quietly. "St. Joseph Street in West Tampa." Sawyer looked stricken.

"A child?"

Sawyer shook his head. "No, it was a woman."

"What?" Talon exclaimed shaking his head. "That's impossible."

"It was the ambulance driver who was taking Derrick back to the home. Everyone is saying he killed her."

Chapter Six

"WHY DO they think it was Derrick?"

Jake itched to soothe Gael, but he had no idea what to do. He felt Gael's thigh pressed against his own in the truck as they raced to the scene. It was a bit of a squash, as they were in Talon's truck rather than the Lenco, having gone straight from Vance's.

"They didn't say," Sawyer said apologetically.

"Are ENu there?" Jake asked.

"On their way," Talon ground out, and took his truck around the corner practically on two wheels.

"What if it was me?"

"What do you mean?" Jake asked Gael.

"I mean, what if I set Derrick off? Talking. What if I kind of pushed a button?"

Everyone in the truck was silent, waiting.

"What do you mean?" Jake said slowly, carefully. He needed to understand exactly what Gael was trying to blame himself for this time.

"We have no idea of his abilities. Any one of us is capable of killing by accident, Jake."

"But not deliberately," Jake emphasized. "And I don't mean that you couldn't; I mean you wouldn't."

"Don't do exactly what we have been accused of for years," Vance said in the quiet of the truck. "You're better than that."

Gael raised stricken eyes. "I wasn't, I mean…oh crap." Gael closed his eyes and buried his face in his hands. Jake itched to put his arm around him.

"I think," Jake said hesitantly, "that you've had a ton of shit to deal with in the last few weeks."

"None of which gives me an excuse for making an assumption," Gael said, flatly. He raised his head and stared out of the window.

"Gael," Talon nudged him. "Buddy, stop thinking everything is your fault."

"He's a child, Talon, and what did I do? Not only assume the worse, but I made it all about me. *What did I do to set him off?*" Gael parroted. "Not what can I do to advocate for someone who can't do it himself." Gael's eyes glinted. "This is exactly why we are here, and I fell into the same trap as everyone else."

Talon nudged him again. "So, let's make sure he has someone in his corner, huh?"

Jake saw the rueful, but determined smile Gael gave to Talon, and then something occurred to him. "Talon, do we know what happened to the other driver?" There had been two when Derrick had been picked up yesterday.

Talon shook his head. "We'll be there in ten minutes" was all he could offer.

It was a circus. Tampa PD, three ambulances for God only knew what reason, a fire truck, and five police cruisers. The only small consolation was that ENu wasn't there. Jake knew they would have sedated Derrick without giving him a chance.

Gael was out of the truck before Talon had even put it in Park, and Jake was right behind him. "Where is he?" He flashed his badge to the nearest cop, and then he turned and looked beyond the sea of police. Ten, fifteen cops all stood in a perimeter around a Chevy Impala. Everyone had their guns drawn. The only occupant, Derrick, sat in the back seat, rocking slightly, his hands clasped tight on something in his lap.

Jake noted the stripes on the uniformed cop scurrying toward him. "What happened?"

"We have no idea, except another car drew up behind this one as the lights were red. When he didn't move at green, the driver got a little agitated and sounded his horn, but there is no room to overtake. After another light cycle had passed, the driver got out. He says there was one driver, a female, and she was staring ahead. He knocked on the window, and at that point, he noticed the child in the back. He panicked and dialed 911. He says he never noticed anything except the child seemed distressed."

"And his scar," Talon said flatly. Because that would be the only reason someone would see a child in distress and not try to help.

Jake nodded to the car. "Has anyone tried to talk to him?"

The cop reddened and shook his head. "The EMTs got the woman out and pronounced her dead. They said from the burn marks, it looked like she was tasered with something. We thought it best to wait for you."

Talon drew himself in; Jake could imagine what words he was fighting not to say.

"And we're grateful you called us," Talon said.

Jake admired his control. He wanted to pin the fucker up against a wall and ask why they were drawing down on a child. He didn't, though.

"Talon?" Gael obviously wanted to go to the car.

"Remember, we don't have Eli," Talon cautioned. Gael took a step, and so did Jake. Talon put a hand on his arm, and Jake merely raised his eyebrows. "You don't touch," Talon ordered and stepped back.

Jake nodded and followed Gael.

"Derrick?" Gael said as soon as he was close. The car doors were open, but Derrick gave no sign he had heard him. "Derrick?" Gael said again, going around to the other side and slowly sliding into the back seat. Jake stayed outside, and when Gael drew a sharp breath, he leaned in to see what Derrick was clutching. His tablet, except it was broken. The screen was badly cracked.

"That must have taken some force," Jake said quietly.

"It makes no sense," Gael agreed and started signing on Derrick's hand. "Hi, Derrick, it's Gael."

"Gael," Jake cautioned, hearing a door slam and seeing Carmichael and three others get out of their truck. Talon strode over to Carmichael, along with the sergeant, and Jake suddenly wondered who had jurisdiction. Technically this wasn't an FBI case, even if it involved an enhanced.

"Derrick?" Gael repeated, signing at the same time, and he raised helpless eyes to Jake when Derrick showed no sign he even knew they were there.

Jake crouched down to be on their level but still stayed outside the car. "Gael, I think we're going to have to let the EMTs take him." He could see Mac getting into it with Talon and wasn't sure how long Talon could hold them off. "How about if we both go with him?"

Gael nodded and signed again.

Jake took another look at Derrick. No response. He was rocking backward and forward slightly, clutching the broken tablet, low guttural noises coming from his throat. Jake had no idea if his distress was because of what he might have seen or because without the tablet he couldn't communicate. He sighed and walked back to where Talon, Mac, and the others were talking to the paramedics.

"I am not about to let some crazy get in an ambulance without putting him out. I wouldn't be doing my job if I let that happen."

"Gael and I will go with him," Jake said before Talon could respond. He could see Talon was about ready to punch Mac. Not that he blamed him.

Mac sneered at Jake. "Feeling guilty?"

Jake's lips parted soundlessly. *Did he know?* His pulse beat loudly in his ears. Vance shot him a puzzled look, and Jake struggled to swallow down his dry throat.

"I'll tell the EMTs," Talon said. "Can you get him out of the car?"

Jake blinked. "Tell them to bring the ambulance close so we have some privacy." He nodded to where a news van had just pulled up. Jake turned and walked back to the car, trying to force his worry down.

Gael looked up as Jake bent down and gazed at them. Gael shook his head. Derrick was still doing the same thing, as if they weren't even there.

The ambulance slowly backed up and both paramedics got out. "Come on, buddy," Gael said and tried moving Derrick toward the edge of the seat. Derrick clutched his tablet tighter but allowed himself to be slid across. Gael got out, glanced at the ambulance, and then bent down, put one hand under Derrick's legs and the other behind his back, and lifted him out.

One of the paramedics pointed to the stretcher, and Gael stepped the few feet to the ambulance and up the back step. Jake put out a hand to steady him. In a few seconds, Derrick was strapped down to the gurney. The paramedic—Davis, it said on his badge—wrapped a blood pressure cuff around Derrick's arm and fastened a small clip to Derrick's finger. At least Davis didn't seem frightened of him. "Sit down, guys," he instructed, and Gael and Jake sat across from the gurney.

"We'll follow you," Talon said and closed the back doors.

"Autism?" the paramedic asked, watching Derrick, who was still making low guttural noises.

"FAS," Jake replied, "but possibly autism as well."

The ambulance pulled away.

"Are you taking him to Tampa Gen?" Gael asked.

Davis shook his head. "We have instructions to take him straight to Bayside Psychiatric."

Gael's eyes widened, and he looked at Jake in alarm. Jake chewed the inside of his cheek. They weren't getting anywhere with Derrick. The hospital would have doctors who would know about Derrick's condition even if they had no experience with enhanced, and to be honest, Jake had no idea how powerful his ability was. Yesterday he'd seen Derrick work an electronic device that had no source of power. The ambulance driver looked like she had been electrocuted. He didn't want to make any assumptions, but until they knew more with the incredible abilities his team had already demonstrated, it wasn't beyond the realm of possibility that Derrick was responsible for this.

He understood how this was killing Gael, but until they found out what had happened, Jake didn't see how they had any choice.

Jake sat quietly while Davis took the finger clip off Derrick. He left the blood pressure cuff on and it inflated every so often.

"What's going to happen?" Gael asked as Davis sat down and started writing notes. Derrick still seemed to be in shock, but it was incredibly hard to tell.

"Well, we're gonna hope its Dr. Maya on call, for starters," he said and paused to look at Derrick. "She's on the pediatric team and one of the nicest doctors I've ever met." He nodded at Derrick. "He'll be in good hands." Davis watched as Gael leaned forward and started signing on Derrick's hand. "What do you know?"

Jake repeated what Mr. Ramsay had told them yesterday.

"That his?" Davis nodded to the tablet.

"It is," Gael confirmed but didn't say anything else. Jake was happy to leave the sharing of information decision up to Gael, and Talon when they got there.

Jake put his hand out to steady Gael as the ambulance turned quickly. Gael's eyes softened in response, and the small smile made Jake very reluctant to let go.

NEARLY THREE hours later, Jake had just gotten bad coffee for all of them from the vending machine when a female doctor came through the doors into the reception area where they sat. Mr. Ramsay and Derrick's social worker had arrived hurriedly an hour ago and had been shown in immediately.

Gael jumped to his feet and the doctor smiled and put out her hand. Gael immediately went to shake it, and Jake was surprised at first when Gael never hesitated. But they were all in uniform and Gael wore his like a shield.

"Agent Peterson? I'm Dr. Maya. Mr. Ramsay told me you have had some success communicating with Derrick?"

Gael nodded and briefly recounted what had happened yesterday.

"Well, we've given Derrick a mild sedative. *Mild*," she emphasized, seeing Gael's face change. "It's been prescribed for him before, and at the moment, we have a very scared, distressed young man who needs help."

"Can I see him?" Gael asked.

She drew in a breath. "Perhaps tomorrow. At the moment, I've said he is not fit to be interviewed by any law enforcement personnel, and I don't think I have an argument to be specific about which ones. Let us calm him down first."

Gael blew out a sigh but nodded.

Talon, who had been quiet up to that point, immediately passed her a card. "Those are the team's contact details. If we can be of any help at all, please let us know."

She took the card and pocketed it. "Please feel free to call me tomorrow. I am just waiting on official permission on how to proceed."

That makes sense, Jake thought. He didn't think Derrick had any family, as he had been in the foster home for a long time, but he guessed they had to be careful.

Dr. Maya smiled and excused herself.

"Let's go back to the office and see if there's any news on the missing driver," Talon said.

Jake frowned. "Yeah, there were definitely two yesterday."

"According to the phone call I just got, it's a requirement," Talon explained. "A Barry Jones should have been in the car as well. Gregory said he would call if he found anything out, but we're to head back to the field office in the meantime."

They were walking to the parking lot when they heard a shout. It was Michael Ramsay, Derrick's principal. He jogged over to them and looked at Gael. "Derrick's getting distraught, and the sedative they gave him over thirty minutes ago is having little effect. I persuaded them to let you sit with him."

Gael glanced eagerly at Talon, and Talon nodded. "Of course."

Jake stepped forward. "Just call me when you want a ride."

The team was quiet as they rode back. They swung by Vance's to collect the rest of the cars and then headed to the field office. Gregory and Drew met them as they walked in.

"Tampa PD located the other driver," Gregory told them, "and he's suspended pending disciplinary action. He's at Bayshore precinct. Vance, you and Jake have permission to speak to him. We have no jurisdiction on this and are at the mercy of the Tampa PD, so play nice."

Talon quickly brought Gregory up to speed on what they knew and where Gael was.

Gregory glanced at Drew. "The PM will be started at eight in the morning, and Dr. Bayer from the ME's office is happy for you and Gael to meet her to discuss her findings. We wouldn't get the report until the afternoon." He turned to Talon. "I have a meeting with Assistant Director Manning, and she wants you there. Finn, Sawyer? Chamberlain Senior High School wants you to come and discuss school admission."

"Huh?" Sawyer blinked.

"Ooh," Finn said eagerly. "A Mrs. Anita Ruiz?" Talon chuckled, but Finn ignored him. "She wants to get our input on a possible admission next year. He's in middle school somewhere in San Diego, but his father is transferring to MacDill."

"How do you know?" Jake asked in amazement.

"An old colleague of Liam's dad. They wrote to Liam two weeks ago, expressing their sympathy. Roman, their son, was in elementary school with Liam for a while before they both moved. I chatted with them, and they're very interested in the team, and his dad is hoping to do some work on enhanced joining ROTC programs at school even if we are a long way from them serving just yet."

"Wow." Jake was speechless. In the space of a telephone call, Finn had probably done more for the future of enhanced than had been done in twenty years, with the possible exception of their own unit.

"Go Finn." Vance whooped and high-fived Finn.

Talon winced when Finn staggered back a little under the force that was Vance.

Sawyer groaned and looked pleadingly at Talon, who just lifted an eyebrow.

"You would rather meet with the assistant director?" he asked dryly.

Sawyer, of course, didn't say another word, and they both headed out.

"We'll take your truck," Vance pronounced, and Jake followed him, glancing surreptitiously at his cell phone. Realistically he knew it would be a while before Gael called. It didn't stop him from looking, though.

JAKE GOT in his pickup as Vance squeezed into the passenger side. He needed to get a bigger truck if he was gonna be working with these guys long-term. Jake glanced in some amusement at the big guy as he fought to get the seat back as far as it would go.

Vance was a ginger. Connie's hair was streaked with gray, but she definitely had some red in there too. Vance reminded him of Damian Lewis, who Jake had been known to have a serious crush on and watched avidly in every episode of *Homeland*. In fact, he hadn't even known the guy was English until he'd seen him on a TV interview. And that accent? Wow. Vance definitely had the whole ginger vibe down; he was just the size of two Damian Lewis's. He wore it well, though.

"I guess you're the go-to guy when the team needs to get sent to any precinct, huh?"

Vance chuckled. "That's because at one time or another, I've had just about every captain around to my house. None of them would dare give me shit. I have three brothers who are cops, although Eric's just got his transfer through to Portland."

"Long way," Jake commiserated.

"Yeah, and my mom's taking it hard because Joanna's pregnant."

"Sister-in-law?"

Vance nodded. "Her folks are from Salem, so I guess I can't blame her."

The silence that followed was comfortable.

Jake saw Vance shuffling a little, trying to give his long legs room. "Sorry it's a bit cramped," he offered.

It didn't take more than five minutes from parking the truck to being seated inside an interview room. Detective Ryker had said they were there to observe only, as Mr. Jones had happily agreed to them being present. "He's scared shitless he's gonna lose his job," she offered as they stopped outside a door. "Though that has nothing to do with us, and he hasn't asked for anyone to be here with him, yet."

Jake followed Vance and Detective Ryker into the small room, and they shook hands and introduced themselves. Apart from a slight widening of Mr. Jones's eyes when he saw Vance, he didn't seem put off by the scar on Vance's cheek. In fact, if Jake had to guess, he would have said it was more to do with his size than the fact that he was enhanced.

"Thank you for coming, Mr. Jones. You understand that we are simply trying to find out why your colleague was on her own in the car with Derrick?"

Barry Jones gulped. He had to be sixty or sixty-five, with gray hair and kind, albeit alarmed, eyes. His shoulders slumped as he let out a breath. "I've been an ambulance driver for nearly forty years," he started. "The last two for Health Transport."

Jake shot a look at Vance.

"It's a private ambulance company that has one of the city contracts," Vance explained.

Barry sighed. "It's my wife."

"Your wife?" Detective Ryker asked.

"Annabel has Alzheimer's," he said in almost a whisper. "Her caregiver never turned up this morning. No explanation, no phone call." He raised tearful eyes. "I'm five months away from my pension. I'm just trying to get there, and then I can quit and look after Annabel myself. Maria knows this." He shook.

Detective Ryker glanced at Jake. "Maria Kelly was the other driver."

"We've been driving Derrick for five months. He's never a problem, ever. So long as he has that little computer thing with him, he just sits quietly. I-I have had a lot of time off because of Annabel. I already had two warnings. One more…. She said she would cover for me. Drop Derrick off and come to my house. I was sure Jenny—that's Annabel's caregiver—would be there by then."

Jake sighed silently. Mr. Jones had likely lost his job by trying desperately to keep it.

Vance moved slightly and looked at Detective Ryker. She nodded her permission. "Mr. Jones? How long has Jenny worked for you? Has she been unreliable before?"

"No," he insisted, shaking his head. "Never. I only can't have her full-time because she has another client that she's been with longer than me."

"So, her not turning up and not contacting you would be unusual, then?"

Jake glanced at Vance sharply, as did Ryker. Vance's careful tone wasn't lost on him.

"Absolutely. I was quite worried, actually."

"Jenny?" Vance prodded.

"Jenny Mathis."

Ryker slid a piece of paper over. "Can you write down her contact details, please?"

Barry nodded eagerly, and when he'd finished, Ryker left the room.

"Have you ever had any communication with Derrick?" Jake asked.

Ryker reentered the room.

"No, never. He never even looks at us. What did Derrick do?" Barry asked, the fear dripping from his lips.

"We don't actually know if he did anything yet," Detective Ryker said before Jake jumped in and said exactly that. She stood. "If it helps at all, I am more than willing to tell your employer you were as accommodating as possible."

Mr. Jones stood also, shook everyone's hand, and shuffled out. Ryker walked with the man to reception. Vance and Jake stayed where they were in case she had any questions for them. She was back in a few minutes.

"I've asked a patrol car to swing by the caregiver's address, but that's more to confirm his excuse for not being there than anything else. There were no drugs in the car, which was my only other reasoning behind an attack. There's a chance we had thugs see the logo on the car while it was at a traffic light and tase Maria. Opportunist. Smash-and-grab sort of thing, and she reacted badly to the shock and had a heart attack."

"Cameras?"

Ryker shook her head.

"Was the window down?" Jake asked, thinking hard.

"No."

"But the door would lock automatically as soon as she drove away. Why would she open the door to thugs? It seems odd, especially with a vulnerable child as a passenger."

"Maybe they didn't look like thugs, but it's certainly worth the question. I'll give Jones a call later and ask him what the procedure would be. I'll let you know." Ryker glanced hesitantly at Vance, as if she wanted to ask a question and took a breath.

Vance cut her off. "All we know so far is that Derrick has certain communication challenges. It is impossible to even hazard a guess at what happened. His enhanced status is likely to have nothing whatsoever to do with the driver's murder."

It was shit and Jake understood all the prejudice and assumptions they had been dealing with for years and couldn't think about how Gael was going to cope with this. Gael had enough on his plate and was already suffering. Maybe tonight Jake could cook. He did a mean stir-fry, or maybe he should be more casual and order pizza. Yeah, maybe that would be better. Although cooking would occupy his hands…. He glanced down at his fingers and curled them inward, feeling the familiar stirring in his gut as he thought about how Gael had responded to last night's kiss.

He moved and cleared his throat. Thankfully there was a quick knock at the door, and a cop put his head in and handed a piece of paper to Ryker.

She stood quickly and looked at them both. "Jenny's body has just been discovered in her house. Her throat was slit."

"Jesus Christ," Jake said.

"Look, I'll call you as soon as I know anything, but there's no way this is a coincidence and it looks a lot better for Derrick."

Because if Jenny was killed deliberately to stop her from going to Annabel's, there might just be another reason for Maria's death.

Chapter Seven

GAEL FOLLOWED Michael—he had asked Gael to drop the formality—into a corridor that opened up into three small bays, each containing four beds. There were children of various ages playing with some toys, and one who seemed to be curled up in a hammock. They walked past two private rooms, both with cots laid out, where presumably a parent could stay. Michael carried on until the end room and pushed the door open. There was a younger guy sitting in the corner dressed in the kind of scrubs one often saw at the dentist or any health care place where there were kids. His top seemed to have a pattern of a cartoon train running around his waist. He stood and spoke quietly to Michael before he left, but Gael didn't hear what was said because he was too caught up gazing at the little boy on the bed.

He was crying. Not in a sobbing, dramatic, full-of-snot way that kids did like it was the end of the world, but silently, like his eyes were filled with so much sorrow, every few seconds a little would trickle out.

Derrick wasn't looking at anything except a blank wall. He had his back turned slightly away from where the nurse had sat. He had his arms wrapped around his middle and was rocking slightly. Gael expected the distressed noise he had heard before, but there was nothing.

"He may not be crying for the reason you think," Michael said carefully. "Crying is often the only way a child can communicate, and we have no idea how the mix of autism-FAS-enhanced is working in his brain."

"Where's his computer?" Gael asked, suddenly realizing it was missing.

"They confiscated it," Michael said regretfully. "Cracked screen. We have been trying a substitute." He passed the small children's electronic coloring device over.

Gael took it from him and examined it, suddenly feeling woefully ignorant and frustrated.

"It's the same color," Michael offered, "but as a comfort substitute, it would be like throwing a favorite teddy bear away and going to any store and buying a new one." He wrinkled his nose and then glanced at his watch. "I have really got to go. We have a funding meeting in an hour."

"I'll be fine," Gael said and perched on the bed carefully.

"Call button there. Video monitoring"—he gestured to a small camera—"and the nurse will make very frequent checks."

"Hey, buddy," Gael said, then shuffled a little nearer. "It's Gael." He signed the last part on Derrick's hand.

He picked the same one he had used before, even if it was partially buried with the other. He was determined to read up on the nuances of Derrick's condition as soon as he got home, but he was sure he'd read that routine was very important.

He looked around the room. A sink, a door that he assumed led to a bathroom, a colorful mural adorned one room, which, under normal circumstances would be considered babyish for Derrick, at thirteen, but with everything else he had going on, Gael didn't know.

Gael kept the signing up for a few minutes. The repetitious "Hi, my name is Gael," as he had done at the school, and with his other hand, he picked up the tablet. It was actually quite similar. He would definitely take the original with him when he went and make sure it was repaired tomorrow. Derrick wouldn't suffer another night without it.

He turned it over and saw the panel that covered the batteries like Derrick's. He froze as the thought hit him.

Batteries.

Could it? Would it make any difference? Gael stopped the signing and glanced at Derrick's face, half-hoping for a noise. Nothing, but the rocking was barely perceptible.

Gael would need a screwdriver to undo the cover. Derrick would have been completely unable to remove them without help. Gael reached into his pocket and tried the edge of a coin. It was a little awkward, but it worked. He pocketed the four batteries and the screws, not wanting to leave them lying around. He snapped the cover back on and cautiously held out the small tablet to Derrick. Derrick didn't seem to notice it at first, but then he made one guttural noise like Gael had heard before.

"Hi, Derrick, my name is Gael," he signed with his free hand.

Gael held his breath as Derrick stopped clutching his middle, and with one hand, took hold of the tablet. A single tear escaped and ran down Derrick's cheek.

When the tablet bleeped, Gael could have cried himself.

GAEL WAS exhausted. Derrick had wiped him out, even though he couldn't wait to tell the team. He couldn't even remember the last time he had slept a full night from when he got the letter from his sister. *Half sister.* He needed to call Wyatt, but Wyatt was visiting his girlfriend's family, and Gael thought he ought to check out Louise first.

And now, on top of everything else, as he walked into the field office, he was nervous. He hadn't been lying exactly when he'd told Jake he could rent a room. He could, and he knew his biggest terror would have been the size of the cockroaches that scurried up the walls.

Or was it? Jake had been quite obvious. A harsh man would have said pushy, and it wasn't like Gael was a virgin. It was true when they said one could buy almost anything. He just had no idea why Jake would have said what he did. Jake was gorgeous. Deep gray eyes he could drown in if he looked for long enough. The intense military cut, and the way he stood at attention without even meaning to. It certainly made certain parts of Gael stand at attention, at least the bits that weren't attempting to melt, anyway.

Oh my God. Gael came to a stop. Did Jake think that because of his scar he was an easy target? That he was desperate? *No, no, no.* That didn't make sense. He might admit to being so sometimes, but Jake was gorgeous. All he had to do was beckon a finger, like every cheesy romance moment he'd ever thought of, and someone would come running. He didn't need Gael.

Gael blew out a long breath. Jake was stunning. Beautiful pin-up girls should hang from those biceps. Gael put the brakes on his thoughts—just because *he* was ugly didn't make "gay" ugly. In fact, it was down-right breathtaking sometimes.

He had spent the afternoon with Derrick, but Derrick had mostly slept it away. Dr. Maya had come in a few times and asked what Gael knew about Derrick, but obviously it wasn't enough. After Gael managed to coax Derrick to eat something before he fell asleep again, his precious tablet clutched tightly, Gael had been all set to call Jake. Then the nurse, who had taken a keen interest in the signing, having done some himself, offered him a ride into town.

"Gael?" Gregory peered at him, and Gael tried to look like he was okay. "How was the boy?"

"He seemed calmer, sir. I'll type up my report now."

"Your team is in the gym" was all Gregory said before smiling and walking away.

Gael let them be for a while as he shot into the office and wrote his report on what had happened. Forty minutes later he walked into the gym and found Vance sitting on a bench and Jake laid flat out on the ground. Gael took in Vance's amused look and Jake's groan.

"You're not supposed to kill your partner, you know," he scolded Vance.

Jake groaned again and sat up. Gael walked to the vending machine and got a bottle of water. He unscrewed it and headed back to Jake, holding it out. Jake grabbed it, tipped his head back, and Gael followed every swallow down that smooth throat. He nearly repeated Jake's groan.

"You staying here now?" Vance stood. "I'm going for a shower, then finishing my report. Talon says we can leave whenever we want so long as he has them for the morning."

"Was the separate gym put in so all the other agents wouldn't see our humiliation every time Vance put one of us down?" Jake asked, still sitting on the floor.

Vance chuckled and walked out.

"Walk it off a little," Gael said, grinning.

"How'd it go?" Jake got carefully to his feet and rolled his shoulders.

Gael shook his head. "Incredible. Humbling. I have a ton to tell you. How did your session go with Vance?"

Jake shot him a level look. "For a mammoth he's surprisingly agile," he said appreciatively. "You gonna work out or did you just want to see me taken down?" He smiled, softening the question.

Gael chuckled and looked over Jake critically. "You feel okay?"

Jake nodded and quipped, "Still standing."

"Vance has gone for a shower now that I'm in here."

Jake's brows creased a little. "He didn't actually hurt me or anything."

"We're never allowed in here on our own," Gael explained, and Jake raised his eyebrows. "It's one of Talon's rules."

"Teambuilding?"

"No. The doc does an awful lot of tests on us, and she isn't sure if adrenaline contributes to our abilities developing." Gael looked behind him to make sure the doors were closed. "The thing with my skin? It happened suddenly when I was in a shoot-out. When the team first formed, it was me, Talon, and Vance, and they didn't really know what to do with us. Vance knew a DEA guy, and he asked us for back up. Everyone just thought we were cannon fodder, I suppose. Anyway, the op went wrong, and Vance and Talon were pinned down."

Jake stilled, waiting for Gael to finish.

"I thought I was gonna die anyway, so I used myself as a shield."

"Gonna die," Jake repeated woodenly.

"Cancer."

"What?" Jake nearly shouted the question and took two steps right up to Gael, raking his eyes over him in concern.

"I'm fine." Gael smiled. "Remind me to bore you with the science sometime. Anyway, my skin became a barrier for the first time, and the bullets bounced off me. More agents arrived and everything worked out okay. They started proper training for us after that."

Jake gazed at Gael. His warm gray eyes seemed to slide over Gael's skin. Gael took another breath, not wanting to see something in Jake's eyes that wasn't there. Jake had gotten a loud *no* the last time he had come on to Gael.

"What I'm trying to explain is why Talon won't let any of us use the gym on our own. Safety. He always wants someone here in case our abilities increase, alter, whatever."

"But I'm not enhanced." Jake said it as almost an apology.

"Doesn't matter," Gael said. "You're part of the team, and Talon doesn't have separate rules depending on who you are."

"And you're sure you're okay?"

Gael suddenly realized how close Jake was. He'd taken another step while Gael was desperately trying to rein in his imagination. Gael swallowed, and Jake's gaze fell to his mouth, staring. Gael's throat was so dry. For a second he wanted to step back in panic, but he was cold, suddenly, and the heat coming from Jake was so inviting.

"I'm not going to do anything that you wouldn't welcome," Jake said bluntly. "I want you to feel safe with me."

Safe? That wasn't the word Gael would use. The nerves in his gut tripled, but the tingles in his groin were fiercer. He ached. Just one more step and they would be almost touching.

"You ready to go home?" Jake asked softly, and every nerve, every doubt Gael had just vanished. If the sudden fire in his gut was anything to go by, his butterflies just had their wings smoked.

Home. That one word was guaranteed to push every one of Gael's buttons. It had always been a place. Somewhere secure. In his head Gael had always imagined a sturdy front door, protecting his space, his heart, strong enough to keep every one of his demons out. But it had always been a thing, a building. Suddenly it seemed like a person.

Jake's eyebrows lifted in inquiry. No, in *invitation.* Had he said something else? Were those lips possibly gonna be used for something as mundane as pushing air in and out and forming words? He took a step forward, and Jake's gray eyes blackened suddenly to the color of coal that stoked his fire. Smoldering... just there.

Gael nearly groaned, and Jake just took possession of his arm and turned him around to the locker rooms. He might have said something about how fast he could shower.

The guys had gone when they walked in. Jake just pointed to the bench and told him to wait, grabbed a towel, and nearly ran.

GAEL SAT down. He wanted the weight off his shaky legs.

He heard the water pound out. Was he mad? Was he setting himself up to get hurt? Gael lifted a hand and carefully touched his cheek, closing his eyes and letting his fingers trace over the disgusting puckered skin. Jake was stunning, and Gael couldn't think for one minute why Jake could even stand to look at him, never mind touch him.

Not that he thought Jake was faking for God knew what reason. Ugly didn't make him blind. He'd seen Jake's reaction and knew Jake was aroused, knew something about Gael did it for him.

"I was worried you might have left."

Gael looked up and focused on Jake. He groaned out loud this time, and Jake's eyes lit up in reaction. "Just get some clothes on."

Jake had nothing on but a towel. Droplets of water snaked a trail down his chest exactly where Gael wanted his fingers to follow. Gael jumped up, needing to move, and ignored the slamming of Jake's locker door, the grunts as clothes and sneakers were pulled out. He didn't look back until he heard the jingle of keys and Jake shutting his locker door. Gael smiled. Jake looked good. Black cargo shorts. Old Chargers T-shirt that fit him like a second skin. Huge, sexy smile that fit him even better.

"Come on," Jake said and held the door open for Gael to walk through. "I left some of your boxes at Vance's, but I think we'd better get the rest inside when we get home." He looked up at the black clouds that were gathering when they got outside.

Gael agreed reluctantly. Rain was practically a given at this time of day in September. Their parking lot was secure, but the back of Jake's pickup was open. He'd thrown a tarp over the boxes that morning, but it wouldn't protect for long against the sort of torrential downfall they got here.

Jake turned off the radio, and they talked casually about mundane things to fill the silence. Not that Gael could have recounted any of their conversation if his life had depended on it.

He looked up with interest as they turned onto 17th Street. "I never knew these were here," he said in astonishment as Jake pulled up along a small row of townhouses. There were five of them, barely a half mile from the Westgate and tucked down a small side street.

Jake grinned. "Colorful anyway."

They certainly were. They were old, kind of squashed together, and each one was painted a different color.

"I swear it was painted like this when I moved in."

Gael chuckled as Jake nodded to the end one. Pink. Gael wasn't sure he'd ever seen a pink house. The one next to it was pale blue. Yellow, green, and orange completed the set.

"Do you rent?"

"Yeah, but it's not exactly cheap around here."

"Nowhere is cheap in Ybor. Even the dump I was in."

"Talon told me he lives in River Heights. Nice old houses. Something with a bit more space." Jake pulled up to the sidewalk and turned off the engine. They both got out, and then he helped Gael peel back the tarp.

Gael stacked two boxes. "I've been looking at Seminole Heights. It's barely a quarter mile away. Same sort of houses, but they're interspersed with low-income housing. Some of the area is a little rough, but you can get a real bargain there."

"Yeah?" Jake unlocked the door and put down Gael's suitcase. He stepped to one side and gestured for Gael to follow him in. "See what I mean about needing more space?"

Gael was impressed. A tiny kitchen island graced a gleaming black-and-chrome kitchen and dining area. There was a small bathroom about the size of a cupboard, and stairs to the next floor. Gael followed him up.

The next floor was nicer, homier. A wider space with a sectional facing a TV, with a window behind that opened up onto a small balcony area.

"The bedrooms are up again," Jake said and continued with the suitcase. Gael followed with the boxes. "It's not huge," he said apologetically as he nudged the door open.

It was great. Yeah, it would be a tight squeeze with his stuff, but it was clean, warm, and he rather liked the landlord. "You sure I'm not putting you out?" Gael glanced at him when there was no answer, and his lips parted soundlessly as Jake's warm gaze settled on him.

"There's room for some of your stuff next door."

Gael smiled slowly and followed the deliberate path Jake took to his own room and pushed open the door. Jake didn't say a word, but Gael could feel his eyes on him as he took in the sparse room. "I wasn't planning on being here long. Too cramped. You can't get a king-size in here, and even if you could, there's the stairs."

He was babbling, nervous, and suddenly Gael was anything but. "A king-size would be good," Gael agreed softly and took a step closer. Before he thought about it, before he changed his mind, before his courage deserted him, Gael slid a deliberate hand around the back of Jake's neck and eased him close.

Jake sighed. A small contented sigh, as if his body was saying *finally*, and he lifted his chin just as Gael lowered his.

It was as good as he remembered. Better. Because this time Gael wanted every taste, every gentle nip of Jake's teeth, every thrust of his tongue. Jake's hands roamed, reached under his shirt, and explored his skin as his tongue explored his mouth. A low sound escaped Gael's chest. Need, want. Simple and oh so complicated at the same time, and he broke off, gasping for oxygen.

Jake trailed a finger down Gael's cheek. "I—" He stopped and took a breath. "Gael?"

Gael gazed into Jake's eyes. The gray was nearly black, pupils swollen with desire, heavy lidded. Jake licked his lips, deliberately, slowly. Gael felt the action in his groin.

"Yes." Whatever the question, that was the answer.

Jake's mouth curled up at the edges, and he let out a warm puff of air that ghosted Gael's lips. "I need you to understand something."

He did? Gael turned his head slightly. Jake's finger had been replaced with the palm of his hand, and Gael pressed his lips there.

"Gael." Jake brought his hand up to catch his other cheek, and he gently turned Gael's head so he was looking at him. "This has nothing to do with you staying here. Please tell me that you understand the two things are different."

Gael blinked and tried to focus on the words rather than the man. He was fighting a losing battle.

"I mean, the room is yours anyway. I don't want you to ever think that one is dependent on the other."

Gael smiled. He hadn't, but later his demons might have tried to convince him otherwise.

Jake's smile softened. "Tell me you understand. Words," he added.

"I understand," Gael repeated. Should he cross his heart?

"Good," Jake said, his voice low and raspy. "Then why do you have so many clothes on?"

Gael stripped his T-shirt off and watched hungrily as Jake did the same. Gael's jeans took longer, his fingers suddenly clumsy. Jake stepped close, and when his fingers brushed Gael's crotch to unbutton them, Gael was afraid he was going to make a fool of himself and come right then.

"Wow," Jake said appreciatively as Gael throbbed against his fingers.

"Get them off," Gael begged, helpless to do anything except grind against his touch. Jake seemed to understand Gael's hurry and his… *need*. Jake wasn't as big as Gael, slightly shorter, but as his large hands roamed over Gael's skin, lips mouthed his neck, and whispered, hot words sank into his consciousness, Gael was willing to swear the man was eight feet tall.

Jake nudged him until Gael felt the bed at the back of his knees. "Steady," Jake cautioned and eased him gently down.

Tears pricked Gael's eyes, and he shut them quickly lest Jake notice. He wasn't used to being treated with such care. Jake's light touch promised so many darker things. Every brush of fingers languid, skin sliding on skin. Jake broke away and reached over to his bedside cabinet drawer. Gael took a few shaky breaths, willing his body to calm the fuck down because at this rate, it would be over before they'd even started. He blinked quickly as Jake's head was turned, but in an instant, Jake was back.

"I'm gonna go real slow," Jake promised, sliding his body alongside Gael's.

Slow? Should he ask? Jake seemed to know what he was doing, but what if he was waiting for Gael to take the lead? Crap. He had before. Every time. Twinks just rolled over and presented their asses like it was a given.... It was just he had hoped... once. He focused on Jake, realizing, as his panicked doubts had been rushing through him, that Jake had gone quiet.

"What is it?"

Gael stared at him. Jake hadn't even taken his shorts off, and Gael was naked. He blushed and tried to pull the comforter over to him, but he lay on it and it didn't budge.

Jake moved so they were face-to-face. He cupped Gael's cheek so Gael looked at him. "Tell me."

"I—" Gael squirmed inside, but he didn't move a muscle.

"You can change your mind," Jake said slowly.

"No," Gael burst out, then just wanted to die. At least it had the calming effect on his dick he had hoped for a few seconds ago.

"I wouldn't expect us to do anything without a rubber. I have my medical—"

"No," Gael interrupted, the desperation loud in his voice.

"Then what is it?" Jake's face fell, and he sat up. He blew out a breath. "I'm sorry, I should have asked."

Now Gael was confused. "Asked what?"

"I don't bottom," Jake said bluntly. "Well, I never have, anyway."

"You don't?" A slow smile broke over Gael's face, and Jake's eyes widened.

"*That was it?*" he asked, and Gael nodded, dropping his gaze. "Let me guess. You're enhanced. One of the most powerful human beings on the planet," Jake said dryly, like maybe the jury's still out on that one. "Twinks are all over you. They're attracted to the power, and they never realize that the real power is in you giving it to them. Or not them, because I'm willing to bet you only want to bottom for someone who has the strength to make you? Even if that's an illusion?"

Gael's face got hotter.

"So you've never—"

"Once, twice maybe. I—"

Jake pressed his finger to Gael's lips to silence him and followed it with a slow, unhurried kiss. Gael felt all his worries start to slide away. Jake trailed his finger down Gael's chest and brushed a nail over Gael's nipple. Gael couldn't stop the sharp inhale and the involuntary arch of his back.

Jake raised his eyebrows. "Like that, huh?"

The sound of agreement from Gael's throat was unintelligible, but Jake seemed to get the message. His smile was wicked.

"Do you trust me?"

Gael stilled. He hadn't made that leap. That the thought of bottoming for Jake made him vulnerable. He searched Jake's eyes and nodded imperceptibly.

"Good," Jake whispered against his ear, and Gael shivered. "Because we have nowhere to be except here, and I'm planning on taking my time."

Chapter Eight

"LOOK AT me," Jake urged, wanting to see the lust in Gael's eyes. The cobalt blue was deep, with blown pupils. His cheeks and neck were flushed, and the lips Jake had just mauled were wet and swollen. He looked beautiful, and every heaved breath, every shudder, screamed the arousal Jake needed to hear. He knelt up and kept his gaze locked on Gael's as he slowly unbuttoned and peeled his shorts down. He knew what Gael had seen as soon as his eyes widened. Jake smiled as Gael's lips parted, and he nearly groaned as he imagined where he would like them to be. He lay down on his back next to Gael. "Wanna take them off?" He wasn't small, and his briefs hugged everything nicely.

The speed at which Gael sat up and got on his knees was very satisfying.

Gael's eyes shone, and Jake's cock pulsed in response. He didn't once attempt to silence the noises spilling from him—the gasp as Gael's cool fingers brushed his overheated skin, the whine when gentle fingers brushed his groin, and the moan of sheer relief when Gael pulled his briefs down and his cock sprang free. His balls were already tight just from the heavy kisses and the noises from Gael. Jake couldn't help the second gasp as Gael smiled in sudden confidence and licked the underside of his dick from root to tip.

Jake fisted his hands. Gael hadn't been intimidated by kissing his groin or giving a cautious nuzzle. He dove straight in and nearly took Jake's head off. Suddenly Gael wasn't the only one who needed to calm down. Or did he? Maybe taking the edge off would be a good idea, make him relaxed.

Jake reached for the lube he had taken out earlier, and Gael watched as he flicked the cap. "You got me too hard, too fast," Jake whispered, figuring putting it all on Gael was a good move. The slow smile was his answer. "Let's just get one out of the way, and then we can play. Maybe get a beer. A pizza? There's no rush." Gael's smile fell a little in disappointment, and Jake cupped his cheek. "I just wanna last, and look at what you do to me," he added, realizing he had put doubt there.

Their lips touched. Gael moaned deliciously and pressed against his body. Jake pushed Gael so he was on his side and then rolled over so they were facing each other. Jake got some slick on his fingers, but with the way they were both leaking, he wasn't gonna need much. He slid his left arm behind Gael's neck and pressed his face close, but instead of kissing his lips, he licked and gently bit his jaw. Jake didn't make a thing of touching his scars because he knew Gael would freak out, even if they didn't bother him. He brought his right hand between their bodies and shuffled so they were lined up. With one hand he clasped both their dicks together, to be rewarded with a full-body shiver from Gael and an inarticulate sound he took as pleasure. Barely five strokes and they were both as hard as steel and as smooth as silk.

Gael stiffened.

"Relax, baby. Feel good?"

"Oh fuck," Gael gasped, which Jake guessed meant yes. One of Gael's arms was trapped between them, and the other tugged his hip as if desperate to close the miniscule gap. Jake attacked Gael's mouth. He set up a natural rhythm that didn't have to be perfect, as it was so good now, he doubted if Gael would last a minute. Who was he kidding? He was right there with him. He smoothed his hand up and down, tightening and squeezing until he broke free of Gael's lips, frightened Gael was shaking so much, he was going to fly apart.

"Jake," Gael cried, squeezing his eyes shut as he thrust into Jake's hand, arching and throwing his head back.

Once, twice, and only because Jake was so lost in the most perfect expression he had ever seen etched on Gael's face did his own orgasm barrel over him out of nowhere and their spunk spurted and mixed, hot and heavy. Jake loosened his grip as a heady daze washed over him. The heat, their smell, satisfying and exhausting all at once. He gasped for air, feeling Gael shaking and doing the same. Another inhale, and he blew it out slowly and opened his eyes. Gael's fluttered open at the same time, and they lay gazing at each other, sated. Gael's eyes drooped, and Jake widened his.

"Hey." He nudged him and moved an inch closer to press a warm kiss on his slack lips. "We need to hit the shower."

Gael blinked in a complete daze, as if Jake was speaking some foreign language, and Jake eased his left hand out from under Gael and sat up. He could still feel Gael's stare, and while he wanted to laugh, maybe go *eww* like a five-year-old at the sticky mess, something told him now wasn't the time for jokes. Gael didn't need humor. He needed tenderness, taking care of, and lots of attention. He didn't think Gael had had a whole lot of any of that in his life, ever.

Jake reached for his T-shirt and quickly wiped his hand and belly. He did the same to Gael, and then bent for another kiss. He loved kissing, touching, hugging. None of the guys he'd dated seemed to be into any of that. But then, maybe he'd just dated the wrong guys.

"I'm just going to run the shower. Then we'll order pizza and get some beers." He trailed a hand down Gael's flushed cheek, deliberately touching his left one this time, but he lifted his finger so quickly Gael didn't have the chance to flinch or pull away. He groaned theatrically as he stood, and he got rewarded with a smile.

Jake walked slowly into his shower room and glanced around in satisfaction. This was really why he'd rented the pink house. There was no bath in here, but a nice big shower. He grinned. Big enough for two. He turned it on and walked back into the bedroom. Gael was tracking his movements, barely. His eyes were half-closed, and he looked sated. He'd heard the expression "well-fucked" but it was too crass a word to use on someone like Gael.

"Come on, sleepyhead." Jake chuckled and extended his hand, which Gael grasped.

"Are you gonna carry me?" he teased.

Jake looked askance. "Do I look like Vance?"

"No." Gael smiled. "You're way cuter."

"I'm not cute," Jake groused and pulled him up. "Men aren't cute."

"Mmm. Well, put on those sexy tightass briefs again after your shower and we'll see." Gael waggled his eyebrows, and Jake put his head back and laughed loudly. Gael got rewarded with a kiss and then a smack on his ass, as he was taking too long. Jake suddenly wasn't sure about bothering with food; he wanted a second course of something else. Gael might be hungry, though.

"Do you wanna do pizza? Chinese? I can cook, but I'm feeling lazy."

Gael pretended to consider. "Go downstairs and cook, mess with chopsticks that take far too long, or"—his voice dropped to a throaty whisper—"feed each other pizza in bed."

Jake blinked as a hot wave washed over him. "Pizza it is."

The shower was warm, and Gael picked up and sniffed the shower gel before Jake deliberately took it from him.

"I got you all messy—only fair I clean it off."

Gael's eyes flared, and damn him if Jake's own cock didn't jump a little in response to Gael's reaction. He squeezed out a generous amount of the soap on his hand. Gael shuddered as he stroked his hands over Gael's chest, neck, and very carefully, his face. Jake had some special scrub for his own face, but he was all for quick at the moment. He could find out in the morning what Gael used when they unpacked his stuff. He slid his hands down over his abdomen and very gently washed his balls, cock, and groin. Gael was rocking gently into his hand by the time he had done.

"Turn around."

Gael blinked as if he was in a complete daze but turned around. He put his arm up on the shower wall and leaned his head against it. Jake made short work of his neck and back, digging in, which pulled some more gorgeous throaty noises from Gael.

Jake wasn't sure if Gael had stood that way accidentally or deliberately, but he was leaning forward resting his head, eyes closed, and his legs apart. Jake picked up the small bottle that looked like soap but was made just for what Jake had in mind. He squeezed some on his fingers and trailed them over Gael's ass. "That feel good, baby?"

He got a deep moan in reply.

Jake traced his fingers down Gael's ass, dipped in between his cheeks, and parted them until he reached his balls, fondling them in his fingers. The speed at which the skin puckered was very gratifying.

"Jake," Gael gasped. "I me…. I mean, I should—"

"Let me take care of you," Jake countered. This really got him going. He loved being the aggressor, but he loved to give comfort, and Gael's large size was satisfying on some basic level that he'd never thought of before. The need to dominate Gael but protect him, see him happy and satisfied, was calling out to Jake so loudly he nearly needed noise-canceling headphones.

Gael shuddered again as Jake brushed over his puckered hole. Jake swallowed down a sharp ache, almost shuddering at the thought of slipping himself between Gael's cheeks and slowly sliding into his hole. The tightness. The heat. He groaned helplessly.

"Have you ever played down there?"

Gael took a breath, and for a second, Jake didn't think he was going to get an answer, but then he heard the small "yes," barely audible over the noise of the water. Jake gave him a kiss as if to say thank you for sharing, and while Gael was briefly distracted, Jake was completely unable to resist pushing the end of his finger inside Gael's tight heat. He wasn't sure which one of them groaned the loudest. His finger was slick and slid right in to the knuckle. Jake reached around with his other hand and clasped Gael's stiffening cock.

"Oh," Gael said reverently almost, as if he couldn't believe how good it was, and Jake gently moved his finger in and out.

He let go of Gael's cock to squeeze some more lube on another finger, cupping and fondling Gael's balls until they felt warm and heavy. He slid first one and then another finger into Gael's ass, slowly, gently. He smoothed his other hand up and down Gael's dick, and Gael cried out, his movements confused, seeming unsure whether to push toward Jake's hand or to move back onto Jake's fingers. Jake squeezed Gael's dick and stroked his palm over the end, which Jake loved himself. Gael stiffened and thrust into Jake's palm, and at the same time, Jake bent his finger and found the small spongy area he was looking for. Gael erupted; his spunk must have hit the shower wall so hard, Jake was willing to bet it had sprayed back on him. He hummed his own satisfaction, even though he was rock hard himself and hadn't come a second time. Later. They had all night.

He quickly pulled the showerhead from its bracket and cleaned Gael, himself, and the glass. He put the showerhead back and turned it off, all the while keeping

a firm arm around Gael, who was dead on his feet. Jake
remembered how every day for the last few weeks,
Gael had looked more and more worried, and the dark
shadows under his eyes had gotten bigger. Gael was
nearly asleep. Jake steadied him as they both got out.
He wrapped a huge towel around Gael and leaned him
up against the sink, briefly rubbed the wettest parts of
himself, and cinched a towel around his waist. Then he
rubbed Gael as quickly as he could. All the while, Gael
just stood completely relaxed with his eyes closed.

"Come on. Lay down, and I'll order us some pizza."

Gael let himself be led to the bed, and he climbed
in and lay curled on his side. Jake couldn't resist a kiss
on his cheek before he covered him with a sheet and
went to crank up the air-conditioning. He was planning on a cold room to provide the need for body heat
later on.

Jake pulled on some clean briefs and sweats and
jogged downstairs to grab his phone and laptop. He
knew Gael had done his report, but he still needed to do
his so Talon had them first thing in the morning. Jake
was five minutes at the most, but when he came back
up, Gael had rolled over onto his belly and bunched a
pillow up under his arm. He was also out like a light.
Jake chuckled and opened his laptop. He meant to do
the report, and he would, but his eyes kept returning to
Gael and how settled and peaceful he looked.

Jake gazed at him and let his brain finally go once
more to what had been bothering him for weeks. Well,
no, not weeks. It had been a year. The worst year of his
life. It was the reason he was in Tampa. The reason he
had left LA. The reason he had joined the team. He just
hadn't expected to get involved with one of them. Had

he made everything worse? He had been trying to make friends before he admitted what he had done, but then he had seen the state Gael was in and he'd just reacted.

And it couldn't go any further. He had to tell Gael tomorrow.

"JESUS," JAKE groaned, opening his eyes, the delicious hot, wet suction on his dick bringing him instantly awake. He looked down and saw his dick slipping in and out of Gael's wet lips. "Fuck," he added weakly.

Gael's eyes crinkled in humor, and Jake fisted the sheet he was lying on in an effort not to thrust his hips and possibly suffocate Gael. Every cell in him was clamoring for him to move. As if Gael knew, his hand clasped the base of Jake's cock to anchor him a little, and Jake lifted his hips in response. Gael just sucked harder, his fingers clenching.

Jake pressed his head back into the pillow as the tingling started in his spine and shot around rapidly to his balls. "Gael, I'm gonna shoot," he warned, and Gael pulled his mouth away but continued to jerk him until his orgasm ripped through him.

Jake's vision whited out for a few seconds, and he heaved a breath, then another.

Gael wiped his hand on the towel that he had been wearing and slid up the bed. "Just so you know, I only pulled off because we haven't talked about it," he said and flopped down. "Not because I wanted to."

Jake smiled, still trying to unscramble his brain cells. "I have a piece of paper in the drawer downstairs."

Gael chuckled. "Same here." He shrugged. "Well, not in your drawer, but you know what I mean."

Jake would have moved if he had any bones left in his body. Currently they resembled the consistency of cooked spaghetti.

They both heard the official text sound on their phones. Jake could have cried. "It's Saturday," he nearly wailed.

Gael got out of bed and looked at the screen. "It's Talon. He wants you to head for the ME's at ten, and then we're meeting at the office at twelve. Apparently Cortes and Ryker will both be present at the PM, but she's willing to talk to us afterward." Gael passed Jake his phone. They were all supposed to confirm to show they had seen the message.

Jake sat up, texted a confirmation, and watched Gael hunt around in his suitcase and pull out a T-shirt and shorts. At least having to change into their uniform meant they didn't have to be in suits all the time, which he thought would have killed him in the Florida heat. "I was hoping to help you get all your gear sorted this morning. Maybe this afternoon if we don't have to stay the day?"

Gael hesitated, and Jake suddenly panicked, wondering if he'd overstepped. Gael might not want to be with Jake all day. Just because they'd had mind-blowing sex—

Did he think Jake was rushing things?

"That would be great, but I've kind of decided, if we don't have to be there long, to text my sister and see if they want to meet up. They're staying at the Hyatt not far from Busch Gardens. Apparently they have a daughter and the vacation coincides with her birthday.

They spent a week at Disney, and they're doing two days in Tampa before they fly back on Monday."

Jake climbed out of bed and went to a chest of drawers to pull clothes out. "No problem." He was relieved. "You know, I'm sure Talon would understand if you wanted to skip this morning."

"No point," Gael said. "They're gonna be in the park until four."

Jake disappeared to brush his teeth and find deodorant, and he heard Gael go into the guest room that had a sink and a toilet. Jake emptied his bladder, washed his hands, and ran his electric shaver over his face, grimacing. He really preferred a wet shave, but he was in a hurry. He took a last look in the mirror and wondered why he did. Not like his face had changed overnight, even if he felt different. He opened the bathroom door to see Gael texting. "I only have the one shower in here," he said. "But whenever you need it, help yourself."

Gael looked up and smiled slowly, and just like that, another wave of heat traveled up the length of Jake's body.

Jake swallowed, and Gael stood, took two steps to reach him, and slid a hand around his neck to pull him in for a kiss. Hungry lips met ravenous ones. It seemed the more of Gael he had, the more Jake wanted.

Gael finished with a squeeze to his arm. "We'd better not keep the boss man waiting."

Jake followed him down both flights of stairs and picked his keys up from the counter.

Chapter Nine

GAEL GRUMBLED to himself as they pulled up at the ME's office. He really, really, really didn't like Drew. In fact, he would go as far to say Drew was an obnoxious dick.

Drew had been pretty easygoing, even helpful, when they'd started. He seemed to have just gotten insufferable after Finn had joined them, although that made no sense. It was always Drew who said he didn't want to join the unit, not that they wouldn't have him. And to be fair, it might just be because Gael wished he was listening to a certain *California boy* with dancing gray eyes and an easy smile. Maybe with some soft jazz on in the background.

Currently Drew was listing all the minute details and procedures on all the hundreds of autopsies he had attended, like an instruction manual. Luckily blood didn't bother Gael; he was the team medic, so that would have been ridiculous. He just wasn't sure about the rest of it. The smell, the sight. He hated horror movies. He wasn't very good with even the slightly scary ones. The line "I see dead people" was the most fucked-up shit he'd ever heard, especially from a child's mouth, and when the boy turned around and he had half the back of her head missing, he was grateful he was watching the DVD. He was sure an enhanced screaming in the middle of a cinema would have gotten him arrested. Not that he'd ever been to one of those either. Before he got the mark, they never had the cash for that sort of thing, and after, he never had the guts. He should be grateful Drew didn't seem to need a participant in the conversation he was having because, with the heavy traffic, it had taken a while to get to UF where the morgue was.

"Gael."

Gael looked up at Drew, and by the exasperation in Drew's voice, he thought he might have missed the first time Drew called him. He took two quick strides to the door Drew was holding open, and they stopped to sign in and show their ID.

"Hi, Agent Fielding." Kathy—according to her badge—flashed her eyes at Drew, and Gael followed her adoring gaze. He hadn't ever thought Drew was particularly attractive. Slim, with reddish-brown hair and pale brown eyes. They just didn't have the same pull as, say... steely-gray ones. Gael nearly grinned. He had it bad, and Kathy was welcome to Drew.

They shared some story about the newly retired medical examiner, and then an office door opened from the corridor. A woman with gray hair and thin wire glasses, and wearing a smart blue suit extended her hand as she walked toward them. Drew introduced him to her—Dr. Bayer—and they both followed her into a nice airy office. Gael took a relieved breath.

She opened a file as soon as she sat down. "Maria Kelly, forty-three. Death caused by cardiac arrest."

"Manner of death?" Drew asked.

Gael glanced at Drew. Wasn't that what Dr. Bayer had just said?

Drew caught his look and launched into an explanation. "There are three determinations on an autopsy report. Manner of death—"

"Homicide," Dr. Bayer said flatly.

"And cause of death—in this instance, electrocution—aren't the same thing," Drew continued.

Dr. Bayer smiled patiently. "And mechanism of death. The reason the person died. Cardiac arrest," she added. "She has clear Joule marks on her neck."

"Can we see?" Drew leaned forward.

Gael ignored him. "Joule marks?" He attempted his best smile. "I'm sorry, you're going to have to give me the dumbed-down version." He ignored the snigger from Drew.

"Joule marks are the marks—pinpricks I think more aptly describes them—where the current entered the body."

"Like from a taser," Gael asked.

"More like a stun gun," Drew said. He flashed Dr. Bayer a smile. "Most tasers don't leave an actual mark."

"Yes," Dr. Bayer agreed with an indulgent smile. "You have done your research, as always, Agent Fielding."

Gael tried really hard not to roll his eyes.

"Postmortem lividity—" Dr. Bayer hesitated. "Blood coagulation," she explained, but Gael got that one, "indicates she died where she sat. There are no exit wounds, so we don't think it was a powerful current or that it was held on her for a long time."

"Just enough," Drew said gravely.

Okay, Gael was officially creeped out and, of course, Drew had to go look. The space was enormous—a cavernous room with at least eight metal gurneys and what looked like a whole wall of fridges. Maria's body was pulled out of one of them, and Gael made himself look.

Drew seemed fascinated by everything. "And there was no exit wound, which would seem to confirm a low charge over a longer time frame," he said, as if to himself.

Dr. Bayer nodded. "The problem we have is human response to electricity is widely variable. What would cause numbness and pain on one individual would kill another." Dr. Bayer gently turned Maria's head to the right. The two small pink circles—Joule marks—were clearly visible just under her left ear.

"That's interesting," Drew said as they drove away. Gael hadn't wanted to hang around any longer than he had to, and luckily neither had Dr. Bayer. Drew, he was sure, could have stayed there all day.

Gael nodded. He was hoping the detectives all showed sense. No stun gun had been found and neither had any other type of weapon. Surely the marks themselves would be enough to clear Derrick? They drove in silence for a few minutes.

"I just want to run in here." Gael nodded to the store as they turned on Columbus Drive.

Drew's eyebrow's rose as Gael pulled out Derrick's broken tablet from the bag, but he didn't say a word.

"ONE OF the nicest ladies you'd ever wish to meet," Finn read from the report on Jenny Mathis. "That's what the mom of the child with cerebral palsy said."

"Who?" Vance asked.

"Jenny Mathis was the nurse who worked for All Health. Her clients were Annabel Jones, Barry Jones's wife, and Polly Jameson, a fifteen-year-old with cerebral palsy," Drew said impatiently, like Vance was slow.

"No, I know who Jenny Mathis is. This is just the first time anyone has mentioned cerebral palsy, that's all," Vance said mildly.

Gael glanced at Talon to see if he was going to say anything, but technically Drew hadn't done anything wrong; he was just being a dick.

They all looked up as Detectives Cortes and Ryker were shown into the room. Jake quickly introduced Detective Ryker to the team.

"We are working the case separately, as we have no specific evidence at the moment to believe they are connected, but we have agreed on the likelihood they are," Cortes explained. "We were hoping to just maybe go through everything so we're all on the same page."

Gael sat up, interested. He liked picking through facts. He didn't always like the broken bodies that went with them.

Drew immediately stood and started listing the points of the case. Gael's eyes crinkled in amusement at Talon, and Talon's lips twitched. It was funny how Drew always seemed to think he was in charge.

Both the detectives looked at Drew, then each other, and finally at Talon. Cortes interrupted. "Agent

Fielding, we know what's in the reports. I'm more interested in what isn't."

Drew came to a halt and frowned, but sat down when Finn spoke.

"You have something else to tell us?"

Ryker shrugged. "It just doesn't make sense. There was a wallet on the floor with no cash but all her credit cards, and records show she withdrew $100 as cash back from Publix the previous evening after she left Annabel Jones. We have people looking at the cameras that are available, but as far as we can see, she just went home. She didn't have an extravagant lifestyle. She owned a four-year-old Nissan Altima. She was unmarried but had recently split from her long-term partner, Elizabeth Scott, who has moved to Miami and has a dozen witnesses to say where she was last night. She didn't gamble. Her internet showed no unusual history. Her Facebook history shows she belonged to a multitude of book groups. She volunteered at two charities. There is no reason to suppose she knew anyone likely to slit her throat."

"Entry?" Gael piped up.

"She seems to have let the person in. Techs are still processing, but the whole thing is weird."

"So, you're saying the murder is just a coincidence?" Sawyer asked.

Ryker tucked a brown curl behind her ear. "I don't like it. Who slits someone's throat for a hundred bucks?"

"There are plenty of incidents where people have been killed for less, Detective Ryker," Drew chided.

"No," Jake said. "That's not what you mean, is it?" He felt everyone's eyes swing to look at him. "You mean because she wasn't stabbed or shot."

"Why would that make a difference?" Finn asked.

"Because slitting someone's throat is personal, vindictive." Jake stood, pulled Gael up, and turned him to face away from him. He put his arm around Gael's neck. "He or she would have had to be standing behind her. Very close."

Gael held his breath, his whole body lighting up as Jake touched him, manhandled him. He just hoped to God no one else noticed.

"It could have been done to stop her screaming," Talon pointed out.

"She had the TV on, and the house next door was empty. The family had moved out three days ago. No one would have heard her scream," Ryker said, shooting an admiring glance at Jake.

Jake took a step back, and Gael sat down. He risked a look at Jake, but Jake was listening to Ryker.

"How tall was she?" Vance asked.

"Only five feet seven, so that doesn't rule out too many people who couldn't do to stand behind her and reach successfully."

"And I'm guessing because someone has gone to an awful lot of trouble for maybe $100, you are looping around to Maria Kelly?"

Gael suddenly had another vision of Derrick in the hospital. So small. In so much distress. Hands clutching the broken tablet.

"There were no contusions anywhere on Maria Kelly," Gael said slowly. "What did the tablet break on? Derrick certainly didn't hit her with it. The only reason Derrick is a suspect is because of his ability, that they somehow think he can channel electricity, and frankly I think it's getting absurd."

"It wasn't him," Jake said abruptly.

"Agent Riley," Drew said condescendingly. "You really ought not to let personal—"

Jake cut him off. "This isn't personal. This is reading *your* report and being a cop for four years." He looked at Ryker. "You'd have to check with the first responders, but when we got to the scene, Gael had to go around to the driver's side to get in the back seat with Derrick, and I stood by the back passenger side door on the other side of him. The Joule marks on Ms. Kelly were on the left side of her neck. Even if they are somehow thinking he had the ability to channel enough electricity to use as a weapon when all he's done so far is produce enough to work a child's toy, the positioning is still all wrong. It makes no sense for Derrick to undo his belt, strike Maria with his left hand or whatever he used, shuffle back to his original seating position, and put on his seat belt. Even if he lost control of an ability, he wouldn't premeditate the attack and the position—it would just happen."

"No, that's right," Cortes agreed. "It makes much more sense for it to have been someone standing by the window."

"I think it's easy to get hung up on the bad press concerning abilities and forget to look at the big picture. In any other investigation, the position of the occupants of the car would have been one of the first things looked at," Jake added, smiling as if to soften the blow. "I spent years watching my dad and his colleagues draw diagrams, take photographs, even run timing simulations."

"We also understand from Health Transport that they have very specific regulations for transporting vulnerable children," Ryker said. "Apart from the rule of always having two drivers, they have company cell phones in every car. Even if they see an emergency situation, they are never allowed to interfere, stop the car, or get out, simply report it. Their first responsibility is to the child. We have also established from the garage that the Chevrolet Impala will lock automatically after a few seconds of setting off. Child locks were standard and working on the back doors. Ms. Kelly would have had to open the door herself.

"Ms. Kelly was an impeccable employee with over twenty years of experience and not so much as a parking ticket," Ryker continued. "Apart from the huge risk she had taken by transporting Derrick herself, we are struggling to believe she would break any other cardinal rule and open the door to anyone."

"Unless the person who asked her to open the car door had a badge," Finn said suddenly. "Think about it. If she was requested to open the door by someone whom she thought was a cop, she wouldn't refuse, would she?"

"No," Ryker said thoughtfully. "No one would."

"There's no chance a cop stopped her and she wouldn't roll down the window," Jake said, the excitement rising in his voice, "which would fit with the marks on her neck, but doesn't explain the broken tablet."

"And the assailant would have had to open one of the back doors to get to it. Seems odd," Cortes mused.

"It seems cruel," Gael said. "But it also might mean it wasn't opportunist. That someone didn't just see the logo on the car."

"I hardly think—" Drew started.

"Are you thinking she was being followed?" Jake leaned forward, cutting him off completely.

"Possibly, but what I mean is, to try and blame Derrick, it had to be someone who knew about the tablet.

How possessive he is of it." Gael thought hard. *Possessive, yes. Linked to his ability?* There were less than a dozen people who knew of that, and the worst thing was most of them were in this room. He caught Talon's gaze and knew instantly he was thinking the same thing.

Gael studied Cortes and Ryker. How did he ask if one of their team might have either told someone or be responsible in the first place? If Gael could have shaken his own head without anyone noticing, he would have. The whole idea was getting far-fetched and out of hand. There had to be another explanation.

"We're also forgetting something else," Talon said abruptly. "The motive."

"Exactly." Ryker nodded. "Why on earth would anyone actually murder someone just so a child would take the blame for another murder? It makes no sense whatsoever."

"And in the other cases, it was the enhanced who was killed, not the enhanced doing the killing," Cortes added.

"Have we established Derrick definitely has no family?"

Ryker nodded. "Absolutely. His mother died when he was three, but he was removed from her care at birth. No other relatives, and no father on the birth certificate. No financial means, if that's what you are thinking."

"Surely all this will mean Derrick will be able to go back to the school?" Vance asked, leaning forward to look at Cortes.

Cortes and Ryker shared a look. "From what we have heard, the Enhanced Protection Law might come into play," Cortes said slowly.

"Meaning?" Jake prodded, noticing the looks they were exchanging.

"No," Gael said, shaking his head. "He hasn't done anything wrong. You can't lock a child away because they are scared of what he might do."

Cortes nodded. "I agree absolutely, but that is exactly what the protection law does. At the moment it's likely he would stay in a locked mental health facility for the rest of his life."

GAEL FELT his cell phone buzz and glanced at it. It was Louise, his sister. Apparently their daughter had fallen asleep and they were heading back to the hotel. They were gonna watch TV for a few hours and then maybe take her back there tonight. Gael was welcome to come over at whatever time was convenient. They were in room 2022.

Gael sat and stared at the phone. Did he want to do this? Did he want the reminder that his mom had chosen another family over him and Wyatt?

"You okay?" The rumble from the side warmed him, and he glanced at Jake. Everyone else was milling around, getting food and coffee.

He held his phone up so Jake could read the text message.

Jake scanned it quickly. "You gonna go?"

Gael shrugged. "I honestly don't know."

"Look," Jake said. "This may be completely out of line, but if you want some company, I'm happy to go with you. Or Talon," he said hurriedly. "Talon would go."

Gael smiled. "You know the group foster home that Finn went in undercover? Well, there was a kid there who has a chance of a scholarship. He's playing in a soccer match today, and they're going to watch."

"An enhanced?" Jake asked, surprised.

"No," Gael said. "Just a kid who needs support." Gael's voice was matter-of-fact, but he saw Jake tilt his head as he caught the mild censure and he understood. It wasn't about the mark. First and foremost, it was about children.

"Maybe we can swing by if it's still on when we're done?"

Gael tilted his head to the side, studying him. "You're sure?"

"Yes," Jake said definitely.

"Is there anything else we can do to help?" Talon asked as everyone retook their seats.

Cortes swallowed his coffee. "Just out of sheer curiosity, do we have any up-to-date numbers of enhanced now?"

Talon looked to Finn for the answer.

"The last registered count took the numbers just over four thousand, but that's mainly school and whatever employment records there are. There might be older enhanced not in the system at all. There is a higher concentration in Florida, but we think that's because of the team."

"Visibility," Talon added in case Cortes didn't get it.

"Of the team?" Ryker asked. "Because you are trying to make a safe space," she qualified.

Cortes looked around the room. "Is this all the team?"

"We have one member who's been on assignment at a hospital while an enhanced child got fitted with a Spider-Man suit," Sawyer said with a totally straight face.

Cortes glanced at Sawyer, staring at him in a quiet, un-hurried way. The snarky comment didn't seem to faze him. "But I thought you all wore Superman ones?" he shot back.

Sawyer dipped his head, like, *sure.*

"Every enhanced gets a human partner?" Ryker continued. Then she grinned and her green eyes shone. "I'm sure there's some way of saying that all PC-like."

"Regular as opposed to enhanced," Drew supplied.

"So, you're just regular, huh?" Ryker quipped straightaway.

Drew stiffened.

"Actually, Agent Fielding is helping us out temporarily. He has his sights set on Simpson's department," Talon put in smoothly. "I don't think he'll be with us long."

Cortes frowned. "That's a hard gig. Good luck."

Ryker stood. "As soon as we find anything, we'll share."

"Likewise," Talon said, standing as well. Both detectives left, and Talon glanced at his phone. "Unless we have other news, I'll see you guys on Monday."

Gael glanced at Jake, and Jake nodded, following him out.

THE HOTEL was large, with an imposing circular driveway to the lobby and reception. Jake opted for short-term valet parking, as Gael said they wouldn't be here long. He could have just shown his badge and left the truck where he wanted, but that would have brought the on-duty manager out in a panic, and they weren't here as cops.

"Anytime you want to leave, just say we need to be back at work. I'll follow your lead," Jake said quietly as they stepped into the elevator.

Gael squeezed Jake's bicep, and Jake wished he could take his hand, but even though they might have had a good time last night, they were far from any sort of relationship.

They knocked on Louise's suite door. A younger man opened the door after a few seconds, his face breaking out into a smile. "Gael." He stuck his hand out. "I'm Kyle, Louise's husband. Come in."

Gael returned the handshake and introduced Jake, saying they were coming via work as if to explain why Jake was there.

They heard a door close and looked up nervously. A woman with long blonde hair scraped into a ponytail and cornflower-blue eyes came out of a room, with a baby on her hip.

"Please, sit down," Kyle said, gesturing to the small table and four chairs. "This is my wife, Louise," he said walking toward her. He took the baby. "She done?"

Louise nodded.

"I'll put her down. Coffee will be here in a minute." He disappeared through the door Louise had just come through. Jake immediately stood and introduced himself, but he felt ridiculous pointing out who Gael was as his sister would already know, so he sat down. Jake searched for something to say as Gael and Louise were both just staring at each other, but then there was a knock on the door and a maid came in with a cart.

Louise gave a weak smile. "Kyle's ordered us an afternoon tea. I saw it yesterday on the menu. He knows I love all that," she added, and the woman smiled and unloaded the teapot, coffee, cups, and then three plates of sandwiches and cakes.

Jake rubbed his hands. "Looks great. What's everybody else having?" he said innocently, and Louise smiled wider and seemed to relax a little.

She hurried to the table and immediately started asking if they wanted tea or coffee. Jake said he'd never had cucumber sandwiches in his life, so he guessed he'd better have tea and try to do it all proper. Louise giggled. Gael looked like he was still trying to force air in and out of his lungs.

Kyle came out of what Jake assumed was the bedroom. "Out like a light," he confirmed, and Louise poured him a coffee without asking what he wanted. Jake liked that. He liked that someone knew their partner so well. He wanted that, and funnily enough, it had never occurred to him before. Maybe it was the cucumber sandwiches, or maybe it was the company he was keeping. Jake tried to send a reassuring look at Gael. He wanted to touch but didn't dare.

Kyle glanced at Louise and then at Gael. "I'm not sure exactly what Louise has told you, but I wanted to say that she only found out about you six weeks ago."

Louise's hand shook as she picked up a cup to pass to Gael, and she put it down, took one breath, and her eyes filled. "I had no idea," she whispered.

"Ah, hell," Gael groused and stood, then quickly came around to her. "Come here." He opened his arms, and she choked out a sob and nearly launched herself at him.

Jake didn't know who was more shocked, him or Kyle. Gael had gone from scared and insecure to a protector in the blink of an eye. Maybe that had been what was missing. Finn had told him Gael was Talon's best friend, his greatest supporter. But Talon had Finn now, and he didn't need Gael so much. It happened the world over. One friend—either girl or boy—would get a new boyfriend or girlfriend, and because the relationship was new and exciting, old friends tended to get left behind a little. If they were lucky they would always be friends, but it would never be just the two of them against the world.

In Talon and Gael's case, it must have seemed that for years, literately. Then things had gone from bad to worse. Gael's new partner—him being ENu—reminded him of all the bad things about being enhanced. He'd gone on the hostage rescue course and another medic one very soon after. Jake doubted that either of those had any other enhanced in them. Gael hadn't really spoken about either of them, so his lack of enthusiasm was telling. Then he had gotten home to find out his mother had replaced them with a new family. Been thrown out of his home....

It was a wonder the man was sane.

Jake caught Kyle's indulgent look at the sight of the two of them holding each other and smiled. Gael had his head lowered, but Jake could see his expression and the smile. Jake loved taking care of others, feeling needed and wanted, but he had to remember Gael had those same needs too. That's what a partnership was all about, really. Taking turns picking up the slack.

"Why don't we sit down and you tell me what you know?" Gael said gently, and Kyle moved so instead of Gael and Louise sitting opposite, they were together.

Louise went to the small table at the entrance to their suite. She picked up an envelope and carried it back over. "Mom was diagnosed with breast cancer three years ago. She had all the treatments, but it wiped her out financially, so Kyle asked her if she'd like to move in while she recovered." She reached out to her husband, and he smiled and took her hand. "Then six months later, she got what she thought was a bad back. She loved to garden." Louise smiled warmly. "I told her she'd probably overdone things, and it took another month before she went to the doctor." Louise faltered, and Gael's arm slid around her shoulders and squeezed gently. "It had come back, and it was everywhere. Within a month they told us there was nothing else they could do. I took some time off from work." She paused.

"You must have a good employer," Gael said. "The little one doesn't look that old, so I guess you hadn't been back that long after your maternity leave."

Jake blinked. He would never have thought of that.

Louise glanced shyly at Kyle. "I married my boss, so my needing maternity leave is kind of his fault."

Everyone chuckled, and Kyle picked up Louise's hand and kissed it. "It was fairly easy. My family owns two restaurants. Louise started waiting tables and eventually became a hostess. My parents decided to travel two years ago, so they left it to me and my sister to keep the lights on."

"Says the man who works seventy hours a week." Louise arched an eyebrow.

Jake was charmed, and he shot a glance at Gael.

Louise sighed a little. "Mom was okay for around two months, and then she seemed to go downhill really fast. She spent her last ten days in a hospice. It was only when I was clearing out the room she had stayed in at our place that I found the box." She pushed the envelope to Gael.

Gael stared at the envelope as if it was going to attack him. Jake didn't know if he should give him some space or not, but Gael picked it up and shook the contents out. Press clippings from when the unit had been announced in March and then whenever they had appeared in the press since then. Then there was a yearbook photo of a young man.

"Is that Wyatt?" Jake asked, making an intuitive guess.

Gael nodded. "He graduated from Georgetown this spring. He's got a few offers, including one to go do his master's at Cambridge."

Jake glanced up quickly from the envelope. Shit, if Wyatt went to England, Gael wouldn't be allowed to visit. Another blow. Jake sat a little closer, until their knees were touching. There. Gael had the choice. If he wanted to move away, he could.

Gael stared at the clippings. "How did you know these meant anything, though?"

Louise just stared at him and slowly lifted her hands to the back of her neck. She unclasped a chain and brought out a small locket from under her T-shirt. "Because this was also in the box." She passed the locket over, and when Gael's fingers were too big, she reached over and unclipped it.

Gael went white, and Jake leaned in to see what he was looking at. There were two photos. Another of Wyatt's graduation picture, and one of Gael—a much younger Gael with no scar and no burn.

"I managed to find out who Wyatt was nearly right away. He stood with his back to Regents Hall." She shrugged. "Two minutes on the internet." She smiled. "You were a little harder, but I put two and two together with the photos. The *Tampa Bay Times* loves you guys."

"And—" Gael cleared his throat. "She never mentioned us?"

Louise bit her lip.

Gael pushed his chair back from the table. "Tell me about her?"

"She was… delicate, I guess." Louise scrunched up her nose. "Dad was a good man, but he spent all his time looking after her. She had no independence."

"That doesn't sound good," Gael said.

"It was her choice. She completely fell apart when Dad died and then started dating again within three months. All the same type. Big, controlling guys. One of them hit her, and at least she had the sense to step back then."

"She never spoke about my dad?"

"I didn't even know she'd been married before. The older I got, the more impatient I got. It was like she was never prepared to fight for anything." Louise sighed. "I once got into a fight at school. High school was real cliquey, and there was a group of girls making life impossible for one of the quieter ones to the extent that she'd started cutting herself. I walked into the girls' restroom and the head bully was flicking a cigarette lighter on and off in the girl's face."

Jake felt Gael stiffen and slid a hand to his thigh and squeezed. Shit, Gael was having all his buttons pushed today.

"I yelled and we started a shoving match, which resulted in Jenna—the bully—getting a bruise. I got hauled in front of the principal and my mom got called in. I knew my dad would have stuck up for me, but Mom just shook her head in disappointment and after said it wasn't my place to get involved. In fact," Louise added, "as far as I can remember, she only did one courageous thing for me ever."

Gael tilted his head.

"Gael? The thing is, I think I'm the reason she left."

"That's impossible." Gael shook his head.

"Do you remember the day she left?" she whispered.

Gael swallowed. "June second, twenty-three years ago. It had been Wyatt's birthday, and my dad had missed everything. He'd come home drunk, and we were sent upstairs but we could hear the arguing."

Louise nodded. "When I found out who Wyatt was, I got his date of birth."

"What's that got to do with anything?" Gael's hand had dropped to his leg, and Jake wound his fingers through Gael's. He didn't like where this conversation was going.

"I'm twenty-three the week before Halloween. Mom must have been nearly five months pregnant with me when she left you guys. Gael, I don't think I'm your half sister. I think I'm your full one."

Chapter Ten

JAKE KEPT glancing over at Gael as he drove back to his house. Gael was quiet. Too quiet. He had barely spoken after Louise had dropped her bombshell. He had made all the right noises, possibly arranged a visit for later in the year, and assured her he wasn't hurt or upset, but Jake knew better.

It was killing him.

It was bad enough that his mother left and never came back, but the assumption was that she had left because she valued the well-being of her unborn child over her current ones. Jake never wished ill on anyone, but it was beyond him how someone could do that, how a parent could value one child more than another.

Jake couldn't see Gael's face because it was turned to the window. The complete crapshoot was that Gael had no one to ask that question to. They would never know if it was choice or something else that stopped her from coming back for him and Wyatt. The only small silver lining was that she had left before Gael had gotten his mark so he couldn't blame himself. Jake knew he would try, though.

"You okay?" It was a silly question, but Jake didn't know what else to say.

Gael turned to look at him. "I can't decide if it's better or worse."

"Because she left knowing she was pregnant?"

"Yes. I mean, that makes things hard. I'm never gonna know why she never came back…. Except, maybe I kind of do?"

Jake gave him a quick glance as they slowed for someone making a right.

"Louise said it herself. She needed a protector and was unable to function without one. The only thing she ever did for Louise was leave, and it could be that he gave her no choice. He might have just told her to get lost, threatened her, and she just wasn't strong enough to do anything else."

"There's a chance her new husband might not have even known about you two. From what Louise said, he was a good man."

Gael nodded. "Thanks for going with me."

"Anytime," Jake said and meant it.

Both their phones bleeped and Gael fished his out of his pocket. "Oh," he said, clearing his throat. "Amy emailed their client list. She's included their current ones and all the old ones going back three years."

"How many?" Jake asked, glad for something else to talk about.

Gael scanned his phone. "Jesus. Over a hundred and twenty that left, but of that, seventeen restarted.

Mmm," he said. "She's noted when a house sale caused the contract loss, so I guess that helps, but even with that, we're looking at over sixty."

"You hungry?" Jake asked when traffic slowed, and Gael finally looked at him. Jake caught his breath at the hurt in Gael's eyes. He was barely keeping it together.

Gael nodded and seemed to shake himself a little. He looked at the clock on Jake's dashboard. "Do you mind if we swing by the soccer match? It's at Manygates Middle. The parents do food for after, and I'd like to go." He paused. "You don't have to stay. I mean…."

Jake put his hand on Gael's knee. "Of course I'm going. Then we can swing by the store and grab something for tonight." He waggled his eyebrows. "I can stir-fry us something? You can show me how good you are with chopsticks."

Gael smiled and covered Jake's hand with his own. "I'm glad you came."

Jake nodded, his throat suddenly too tight to respond.

LIAM CAME running over with a few more kids as soon as Gael and Jake got out. "They won." Liam grinned.

Gael high-fived him. "Sorry we missed it."

"It's okay," Liam assured him. "Vance recorded the highlights on his phone."

Gael's smile was huge, and Jake realized it was a good thing, them being here. If they had gone home, Gael would have retreated further. But no one could be around the kids and not have their enthusiasm rub off.

Jake was introduced to two foster kids named Lee and Alec. Apparently Liam had made friends with them in foster care before he went to live with Connie. Then he met two other kids, Aaron and Paul, both enhanced and both equally pleased to meet him. They all ran off for burgers when Finn yelled for them.

Jake took in the parents and the regular kids all milling around. He waved at Connie when she spotted them. No one seemed concerned there were three enhanced kids here, to say nothing of the enhanced adults.

"Manygates Middle is one of Connie's schools," Gael supplied.

"She's a teacher?"

He chuckled. "No, she's been a foster mom for over twenty years. Liam's her first enhanced, but she has a lot of respect among the teachers at half a dozen schools, which Vance could name for you. Inviting Liam's enhanced friends will have been deliberate on her part. She's on a mission to prove that enhanced aren't scary, and she says it starts with the kids."

Jake watched as she handed out small cartons of juice from a cooler. Sometimes moms made the best commanders-in-chief in any battle, and he suddenly missed his. He'd let his dealings with his dad color how he felt about his mom. Maybe he would give her a call. She'd left him a voicemail asking how the new job was going nearly a month ago, and he had been angry enough to ignore it.

Vance called over to them, and they walked to where he seemed to be in charge of flipping burgers. Jake's belly growled. Talon smiled and joined them, and Jake stepped over to Vance, giving Gael and Talon some time to talk. People were finishing up and starting to head to their cars.

Sawyer stood sipping from a can of Coke, and Jake widened his eyes in surprise as he saw Detective Cortes in jeans and a T-shirt, talking to Sawyer and a woman Jake didn't know.

Vance followed his gaze, handing Jake a paper plate with a burger on it and pointing to a small table with napkins and ketchup. "He turned up about an hour ago. Apparently he has a nephew here."

"Who's the woman?"

"Teacher. She's nice. Had a tough deal with a student last year, accusing her of molestation. My dad knew the family and got the whole thing sorted out."

"That's rough," Jake said and watched her smile at something Sawyer said.

"Yeah, the kid was being molested, but it was going on at home." Vance sighed. "Accusing the teacher was an attempt to cover it up. She'd been giving him extra help after class because she'd noticed his work was suffering."

Jake frowned. "How's the kid?"

"Rehomed with his elder sister," Vance replied.

Jake watched as more parents started to take their kids home and a few more cleared things away. "Oh God," Jake mumbled in appreciation around a mouthful of food.

Vance chuckled. "Never, ever, skimp on the meat," he said, waggling his finger at Jake. "You need to come around to my place when Daniel is cooking. He mixes this glaze." Vance shook his head as if to say it was amazing.

"And he refuses to tell any of his brothers what's in it," Gael said, coming up to get a burger from Vance. "Drives them all nuts."

Vance grinned and turned off the grill.

"They've got a bet going on who can figure it out." Talon squinted at Vance. "Isn't the pot like at $400 or something, now?"

Vance grunted in disgust.

Jake swallowed his last mouthful in regret and looked over toward the rapidly emptying parking lot.

A cop got out of a patrol car and advanced on them, but he was all smiles. Vance introduced Jake to Chris, one of Vance's brothers and a sergeant in the TPD. They swapped war stories for a few minutes until Jake realized that nearly everyone had left.

Liam came running over on his own this time, and Chris ruffled his hair and said he had drawn the short straw and was giving him a ride home. "In your car?" Liam's eyes were huge, and Chris grinned and started walking him to a black-and-white in the lot.

Jake watched and then stiffened as a black Buick rolled into the parking lot and Gerry Atkinson jumped out followed by Carmichael. "What the hell?" he got out, and Vance looked over, but before he could speak, a boy from the other school's team ran over to the car and Gerry grabbed him and enveloped him in a hug. Jesus, Jake hadn't even known Gerry had any family.

"Yeah," Talon said, coming to stand beside Jake. "That's Mark, Gerry's nephew. Gerry's brother died a little over two years ago."

"I didn't know, but they were never real friendly, and I was barely with them two months."

Talon blew out a breath. "You aren't missing anything. Gerry's got a mean streak. Mac's just a bully, but Gerry? You have to watch him."

Jake frowned. He knew Gerry was Mac's right-hand man and would always shoot first, ask questions later, but he'd never really been able to separate him from the rest of the douchebags.

"Gerry had an older brother, Carl, in the NYPD. They got called to a robbery, and the guy just lost it and emptied his gun on the owner, Carl, his partner, and finally himself."

Jake winced.

"Shooter was enhanced. Weird ability, according to his family. He was like a human lie detector. Anyway, he did insurance claims for a big New York based company. I mean, knowing someone was lying? Pretty useful thing to have around insurance."

"I'll bet," Jake said appreciatively.

"Yeah, but get this. His star's on the rise and he gets invited to the boss's house for a garden party. He starts talking to a group of people he didn't know that well, drinking a little too much, and they start a game, like asking stupid things and he has to answer if it's right or wrong. He's showing off, life and soul of the party, and then this woman says, 'Is it true my husband is having an affair with his assistant?'"

Jake's mouth dropped open. "He didn't." He knew what was coming.

"Yep. Confirmed it straightaway. His boss's wife filed for divorce the next day, and the shooter lost his job. Trouble is, the boss was vindictive and blacklisted him. Couldn't get a job to pay for the swanky apartment, and too proud to ask his family for help. Fast forward three months and Gerry's brother gets shot."

"By an enhanced." Jake rolled his eyes. "That's screwed-up."

Talon didn't answer, and Jake looked back at the now-empty parking lot, except for the Buick. As they were watching, Mac and Gerry stared at them and started walking over.

"Talon," Finn said in a low warning, but Talon shook his head.

"They're not gonna start anything here."

Jake wasn't as confident. Then he took a breath. Gerry and Mac were both looking at him. "I got this, guys," he said.

"No," Talon repeated evenly. "You're one of mine. I've got this."

"HEY, JAKEY-BOY," Mac called as soon as they were closer. "How you settling in with your new team?" Jake sighed. On the face of it, Mac was being friendly, but he heard the faint mocking lilt in his voice. "I guess with your experience, you should fit in with a bunch of murdering misfits."

There was a beat, but the only thing Jake heard was his heart thumping loudly against his ribs.

"Look, guys, we're at a school for fuck's sake," Talon began, and Mac eyed him.

"You're that desperate you let anyone on your team, huh?"

Gerry sniggered. "Yeah, don't turn your back."

Jake didn't know how he was still standing upright.

Talon was talking. He couldn't process the words, but Mac and Gerry weren't backing off, even if they had backed down a little.

"What are they talking about?" Gael asked, stepping alongside Jake, the words riddled with confusion.

Jake couldn't have said anything even if he had known what to say. He was too distracted by the very real possibility that he was going to vomit Vance's burger back up. He could nearly taste it, bitter in the back of his throat.

Gerry's eyes widened as he heard Gael's question, and his grin was evil. "You don't know?" He waggled his eyebrows.

Mac snorted. "Some partner you've got there, Peterson, and to be honest, with his track record, I'm surprised they let him anywhere near you rejects. But then, if he can shoot some of you here like he did in LA, all well and good."

Jake wanted to breathe. He just couldn't remember how to inflate his lungs. Like his body was on pause. There was movement, words, all going on around him, but it was as if he wasn't really there.

"What the fuck, Riley?"

Jake jerked. Sawyer, an angry Sawyer, was standing in front of him.

"Not here," Talon ground out, and Sawyer swerved around.

"You know, don't you?"

Talon's eyes met Jake's. Yeah, he knew. Of course he did. There was no way Jake would have joined the unit without the team leader knowing all his shameful history.

"What do they mean?"

Jake's gaze fell on Gael. The short blond hair that he would have liked to be just a little longer to latch on to. The smoky blue eyes that deepened and had clouded over last night. The wide lips that were the softest he'd ever tasted. The stubble-covered jaw, because maybe sometimes he had to shave twice a day, and the pulse point beating in his neck. The exact point that

Jake had rested his own lips against and wished the heart that was beating belonged to him.

He took a step forward, but Gael's eyes widened and he backed up.

"What do they mean, Jake?"

Jake tore his eyes from Gael's stormy ones. He didn't want condemnation to weaken the last memory of them, when Gael was sated and replete. Gael had been so gorgeous.

Vance, Talon, Sawyer, and Finn all stood there watching them. Connie had retreated and was talking to some lady. Gerry and Mac had gone back to their truck. Jake didn't know whether the privacy was by accident or on purpose, but delaying the explanation by getting in a car would be worse.

"I spent four years on a SWAT team, as you know. The last op our team was called to was a report of an enhanced who had gone crazy in a shopping mall. Reports of explosions, multiple casualties. When we got there, it was chaos. People shouting. Fire. A lady said there was a man standing in the middle of a kids' toy shop holding some sort of device in his hand and screaming at everyone to be quiet. There were customers, children, trapped between him and the door. We raced into the store just as the guy turned around and held up what looked like some sort of trigger switch." Jake's voice caught, and he struggled to get air into his lungs so he could speak.

"Steven Shaughnessy. Seventeen," Talon said quietly. "He'd transformed just then in the middle of an argument with his father about wanting the latest game system. Not only is he only the second child we think to have ever transformed while awake, he is the oldest to transform, as far as we are aware."

"I didn't know," Jake whispered, the horror eating at him. He had been a child, and he was dead because of Jake.

"Because you didn't wait to find out," Sawyer sneered.

"Look," Talon said. "Jake was exonerated. It was complete shit, but he was following orders."

Jake begged Gael silently. They stood amid the tatters of guilt, recrimination, and regret. It wasn't fair. It wasn't fair that a child had lost his life. It wasn't fair that a scar could make people lesser than others, and it definitely wasn't fair that just when Jake thought he might have found a new life, it was being ripped away.

Vance, who had been quiet up to that point, stepped forward and handed Gael some keys. "It's in the lot. He did it straightaway as a favor."

Gael wrenched his gaze from Jake's and took the keys. Sawyer made a disgusted noise and started walking away. Vance turned around as Connie walked over, and they finished packing away some leftover food.

Talon glanced apologetically at Jake, then looked at Gael, who stood frozen, holding his truck keys. "If you need somewhere to crash, you know where we are."

They were all giving Jake and Gael the space to process this. Finn opened his mouth but shut it at Talon's look, and they both walked to the lot. It was just him and Gael.

"Why didn't you tell me?" Gael said, still not meeting Jake's eyes.

"Gregory said to give you time to get used to me first."

Gael looked up, incredulity written all over his face. "And fucking me? Was that the easiest way of getting me used to you, or just the fastest?" Pain made the words sound raw on Gael's tongue.

"Gael…," Jake pleaded and took another step.

Gael held up his hands. "No. I could forgive the shooting. I'm not stupid. We live in a world where a lot of shit happens and an out-of-control enhanced could have killed a lot of people. Am I sorry for him? Of course I am. There are way too many children who suffer at the hands of those supposed to be protecting them, and I don't even mean just those with a scar on their faces." Gael heaved a breath as if starved for oxygen. Jake would have given him all he had right there. Gael's eyes narrowed. "Did you think it was funny? A pity fuck to keep me quiet? Amenable until you'd gotten your place on the team?"

"Gael, no!" Jake begged. "I would never—"

He touched Gael's shoulder just as Gael turned away from him. Gael was still not as fast as him, but he was stronger. Fuck, he was stronger. Jake had a split second to decide not to duck and avoid the fist that Gael swung at him in anger and desperation, because he deserved it, and then he connected and Jake went down. The pain erupted in his jaw just as everything went black.

GAEL STOOD completely still, stunned at what he had done, and stared at Jake, lying six feet away on the ground in a heap.

"Gael!"

Gael heard the shout from the cars and saw Talon and Vance running back to where he was.

"Shit," Talon swore, falling to his knees. He put a hand to Jake's neck to feel for a pulse, the relief in his face obvious when he felt one. Talon quickly stood, ifting an unconscious Jake in his arms. "For fuck's sake, Gael. What were you thinking? You know we're much stronger."

A squeal of tires announced Finn driving up in Talon's truck. He looked at Vance and Connie. "Vance, follow us. I'm taking him to Tampa Gen."

Vance held the door open while Talon slid into the back.

"Gael, get your ass in here."

"We'll follow," Vance shouted and bundled his mom to the truck, Connie hurrying to get in, everyone staring at Gael like he had killed someone. His heart was pounding, but it was the only thing in his body capable of movement. For a second he met Talon's gaze, and then he turned and did the only thing he could.

Run.

Chapter Eleven

WHAT DID I do?

Gael fisted his hands to stop them from shaking. He was a coward. He hadn't even waited to see if he'd badly hurt Jake.

They were stronger. That was originally why they had brought Drew in to spar with Finn. Him and Talon could easily kill a regular human, and Vance? He could probably take out an army.

He had meant to hurt. Everything in him at that second wanted to blame Jake. Blame him for Gael thinking he had found someone who didn't see the scars, or perhaps someone who saw the scars and still didn't care.

Gael blew out another breath. He was sitting in his truck outside the phone repair shop. The meter for the parking had long since run out, but Gael didn't seem to be able to move. The expression on Jake's face was running in a constant loop in his head. He'd seen Gael swing. Gael was stronger, but Jake seemed to have instincts that Gael didn't, and he knew Jake could have gotten out of the way. For an instant he had caught the sadness in Jake's eyes, the apology, and knew he deliberately stood and took the punch. Gael had finally found someone who didn't seem to think he was a monster, and what did he do? Behaved exactly like one.

He clutched his phone tighter. Carefully, slowly, he texted a message to Finn. He was too ashamed to ask Vance and Talon. He was sure the censure would have been apparent in the reply.

It took the longest time, and when it got to the point where Gael thought his heart would pound out of his chest, he got a reply.

Concussion. Awake. No permanent damage.

Gael took a shaky gulp of air because he had stopped breathing and hadn't realized. His phone bleeped again.

He's asking for you.

Shit. Gael silenced his phone and stared at the text. Jake was asking for him? Gael's first thought a few moments ago was right. He *was* a coward. He could no more walk into Jake's hospital room, knowing he had put Jake there, than he could run into a burning building. No, that wasn't true; the burning building was doable.

He took another breath and started the engine. He could take Derrick his mended tablet back and visit with him for a while. Assuming he was allowed. Gael pulled away from the curb, and the car coming up alongside him nearly took the fender with it. Gael cringed, held up his hand in apology, and took the barrage of insults offered by the guy driving the minivan.

The next attempt was better. At least the only collision now was his heart against his ribs.

"FUCK." JAKE accompanied the curse with a pathetic moan and opened his eyes. His jaw had to be broken, and he felt like his head had split in two.

A large hand settled on his, and for a second, tears pricked his eyes until they focused on Talon. Disappointment hurt more than the fist.

"You look like shit," Talon said flatly. "They reckon concussion but no permanent damage."

"T," Finn admonished, pushing him out of the way and pressing the button on a small controller that tilted the mattress up a bit. Finn reached for the glass and straw on his bedside table and solicitously offered it for Jake to take a swallow.

Jake cracked his eyes open a little more as his stomach rebelled a little at the water. He saw Vance sprawled in the chair in the corner, regarding him steadily. Finn and Talon were the only others there. He sighed before he could pull back the reaction.

"I'm gonna break a confidence," Talon said slowly.

Jake squinted up at him, trying to keep him in focus.

"You know Gael's mom left him when he was six? Well, he transformed when he was eleven, and his dad, already a complete shit, got even worse. He was a drunk. Gael spent all his time either keeping out of his way or keeping Wyatt out of his way. His school attendance was spotty even before the mark. Anyway, one morning before school, his dad caught Gael standing on a bathroom stool, trying to cover the scar with some old makeup his mom had left that his dad had never thrown away. He was getting shit at school for it every day, but even worse, Wyatt was getting it too. His dad was drunk, hungover, whatever, but this time he went psycho on him. Screamed if he wanted to cover it so badly, he would help. He had one of those handheld gas lighters for the stove in the kitchen, and he pinned Gael down and held the flame to his cheek."

Bile rose in Jake's throat and he grabbed weakly at some tissues.

Talon squeezed his arm, and he waited a few seconds. "Neighbors called the cops because of all the screaming, but Gael was convinced him and Wyatt would get split up in care, so he said he'd done it."

"And they believed him?" Jake was aghast.

"Early days of enhanced, ENu. There were quite a few injuries caused by people trying to cut the scar away," Talon answered bluntly. "That's why he has the scars, and that's why he is convinced no one could like him just because he's a good guy. He's convinced they will always see the scars. He's used to people being scared of him, being disgusted, so when those ENu bastards said what they did, Gael immediately thought he'd been used, that you couldn't possibly be with him because you genuinely liked him. I guess I have to take some responsibility, because I knew and I didn't tell the team. I'm just getting used to the whole leader stuff, and I'm gonna make some mistakes."

"Talon, you weren't given the option," Finn said and smiled slowly up at Talon.

Jake stared. Fuck, but he so wished someone would look at him like that. No, not just someone. The ache in his gut had a much more specific person in mind.

He picked up the glass again and sipped his water. Just then a nurse bustled into the room and checked his vitals, responses, name tag, and then held out a small plastic cup with what looked like two horse pills in it.

"I'm not taking them," he said decisively.

She frowned. "Mr. Riley, I'm willing to bet your head feels like it's going to explode."

Jake remembered not to nod. "Yeah, maybe, but I'm not staying, and I need to be able to walk out of here."

Her mouth dropped open. "Not staying," she parroted.

"Nope, so bring me whatever you need me to sign."

She threw her hands up, muttered something Jake was sure wouldn't be complimentary, and turned on her heels to walk out.

"Are you mad?" Finn asked.

"Possibly," Jake allowed. "Has anyone managed to get him on the phone?"

Vance shook his head. "Going to voicemail," he said, not making any attempt to pretend he didn't know who Jake was talking about.

Jake squinted at the clock on the wall. It didn't take a crystal ball to know where he would be. "I don't suppose anyone would give me a ride to Bayside Psychiatric?"

Talon grunted. "Like we would let you go on your own."

THE SAME nurse from the previous day was sitting with Derrick when Gael arrived. Gael showed the doctor on call the small tablet he'd had repaired, and he was allowed through with it. Dr. Maya had approved him as a visitor.

Isaac, the nurse with the train pattern on his scrubs, was in awe when Gael explained what Derrick had done with the computer. Derrick stared straight ahead, as usual, when Gael perched on the bed, and Gael immediately started signing, "Hi, my name's Gael" on the back of his hand.

"Where's the other computer tablet he had?" Gael asked, passing over the mended one he had brought.

"One of our other patients wanted it, and Derrick was asleep," Isaac said apologetically, but Gael got it. Derrick wasn't the only child who needed help.

Gael laid the tablet next to Derrick and talked quite conversationally to him. He stopped for a second as his fingers were cramping. "You gonna say hi, Derrick?"

Isaac came closer to the bed, and Derrick did a little head tilt, but because his eyes weren't focused, Gael didn't know if he was listening or had noticed Isaac. Derrick reached out and touched the tablet.

The tablet bleeped, and Gael tried not to laugh stupidly. Actually, he wanted to grab Derrick and hug him, but he didn't know how that would go down, so he didn't.

"Hi, Gael. FBI."

"That's amazing," Isaac said in awe, standing closer to Derrick.

Gael chuckled. "This is Isaac," he said and signed.

"Train."

"Train," Gael repeated and looked at Derrick. *Train?* "Train?" he asked, signing the word as well.

"Derrick. Train."

The door opened and Derrick's supper arrived. Isaac left to take his own meal break.

Derrick let Gael feed him the meatloaf and mashed potatoes, even though Gael knew he could do it himself. Gael kept up the chatter, although he couldn't keep signing as well. Derrick didn't say anything else, but he looked content enough. After he had finished, Isaac returned, helped him to the bathroom, and gave him two tablets, which he swallowed obediently.

"Sedative?" Gael asked, trying to keep any opinion out of his voice.

"Mild," Isaac replied, showing Gael had failed spectacularly.

Isaac fussed around the room, disappeared for a few minutes, and then brought Gael coffee in a white vending machine cup with a lid. Gael thanked him and sipped slowly. Isaac dimmed the lights in the room. He nodded at Derrick, who was lying back against his pillows and yawning. "Let me know when you leave so I can come and check on him."

Gael signed lazily on Derrick's hand, more so Derrick knew he was there than for any expectation of a reply. The tablet was on the bed beside him, but Derrick hadn't even looked at it for at least an hour. Gael sat and watched Derrick's eyes droop and then close. In another few minutes, he stopped the signing.

It seemed odd for Derrick to use the word train, but it wasn't as strange as Derrick writing FBI after Gael's name. Gael looked around the room and stood. Then he smiled. *Isaac*. Of course. He had pictures of cartoon trains running around his scrubs. Gael would bet anything that was what Derrick had seen.

Gael said goodbye to Isaac and the other nurses, told them he would do his best to visit again tomorrow but to please call him if Derrick got upset over anything.

A nurse buzzed the door so Gael could get out of the unit into the reception area. Should he call Talon, rent a room, or spend the night in the truck? Gael was still trying to decide when he looked up and stopped.

Finn, Vance, and Talon were sitting on chairs, all smiling at him. Jake was lying with his head on Finn's lap and looked fast asleep.

"What the hell?" Gael whispered, eyes focused on Jake.

"He's concussed. You need to—"

Gael held up a hand to shut Finn up. He knew what to do. "Why isn't he in the hospital?"

"Because he's as much of a stubborn bastard as you are." Vance yawned and stood. He walked over to Jake, went to shake his shoulder, and sighed. "Go get in the damn car, and I'll pass him to you."

Gael nearly ran to his truck. He opened the door, turned the engine on, and scrambled inside, ready to take Jake from Vance. Vance lowered him into Gael's arms and put his legs on the seat. Jake grunted but didn't open his eyes. Gael gingerly felt over his scalp, but didn't find any obvious lumps. His jaw, however, was a different story. Gael could already see the red and purple shadowing on his face.

"Jesus, I'm sorry." Gael's voice caught.

"You should take up boxing," Jake muttered, then hissed a little when his mouth pulled in a smile. "Where are you taking me?" he mumbled.

"Home," Gael promised.

GAEL MADE Jake wake up when they got to his place. He wanted to see exactly what Jake's pupil reactions and his verbal responses were. Vance helped Gael get Jake upstairs.

"They said he wasn't allowed ibuprofen, just Tylenol," Vance said as Jake groaned pitifully.

"They won't if it's a suspected concussion," Gael answered. "He can't have anything that increases the risk of bleeding."

Talon put Jake's phone and wallet on the nightstand. "You call us if there is anything you need," he instructed. "I won't call the team in unless there are any developments, but either way, Jake definitely is off tomorrow, and I don't want him on his own. How was Derrick?" Gael followed him back downstairs and smiled a little, explaining about the word *train*.

"Maybe his eyesight isn't as bad as they think? I mean, if he can see things like that."

Gael nodded. "Communication is the biggest problem. I'm thinking if we get to where he can say some things to me, maybe I can go with him next time he has his eyes checked out."

Talon paused and looked at Gael. "Let's hope he's allowed, huh?"

Gael swallowed because Talon was right. If they decided Derrick was unsafe, he might never see the outside of Bayside Psychiatric again.

Gael locked Jake's front door and ran back upstairs. Jake was in exactly the same position as he had left him, his arm thrown across his face. Gael turned off the overhead light and switched the small lamp on. Jake sighed.

"Hey, take these."

Jake groaned, rolled onto his side, and came up on one elbow. He looked at them suspiciously.

"They're just Tylenol."

He grunted, swallowed them, and took a few large gulps of the water Gael held out. Then he lay back down.

Gael immediately started unlacing his sneakers and pulled them off. "You need to get your clothes off, Jake. Do you want me to leave you for a few minutes?" He took the pitiful whine as his answer and pulled off Jake's socks, took a breath, and pulled down his jeans. Jake never moved. Gael got a T-shirt out of the closet and nudged Jake until he rolled so Gael could get his shirt off and the T-shirt on. He covered him with a sheet and looked at the clock. There wasn't even a chair in here, and there was no way he was going to another room.

"I know you don't want to, but the bed's big enough so I won't touch you."

Gael swallowed. He'd thought Jake was asleep. "I need to keep checking on you." He came and sat on the bed, and Jake didn't open his eyes as it dipped. "How's the head? Can you open your eyes for me?"

Jake squinted at him, and Gael caught his breath. He'd always thought them gray, but just then, with the low light from the lamp, they could be silver. Long black lashes framed them and lowered, then raised as Jake tried to widen his eyes. "There's one of you, no weird colors, and you're not fuzzy. I was nauseous earlier, but I've just got the headache from hell now."

"You've had a concussion before," Gael acknowledged quietly. "You're gonna hate me because I'm going to have to keep doing this." That wasn't what he wanted to say. He needed to say so much more. "I—"

"Can we leave the inquisition until tomorrow?" Jake said wearily. He didn't wait for a reply, just closed his eyes. "And get in bed, huh? I get why you're here, and I'm certainly not in any condition to touch you."

Gael pressed his lips closed so he wouldn't blurt anything else out. He went into the other bathroom and brushed his teeth. His clothes were still in the suit-case. Pathetic. By the time he came back, Jake had rolled on his side, and Gael was pretty sure he was asleep. He set his phone alarm for two hours and got in bed, completely convinced he wouldn't sleep. He stared at Jake's back, and even as his fingers ached to touch Jake, he knew he'd blown whatever chance he might have had.

Chapter Twelve

GAEL HAD been awake for a few minutes, but he didn't dare move. He wasn't sure how it had happened, but sometime in the last hour since he had woken Jake to check he was okay, they'd both fallen back to sleep and moved.

To each other.

Gael was lying on his back, Jake on his front, but his left arm was slung across Gael's abdomen as if to anchor him, and he was using Gael's chest as a pillow. Gael swallowed. He didn't know whether to move slowly or to move quickly.

Jake sighed and moved his head a little. Gael froze. So did Jake. He must be awake, then, and Gael figured he had nothing to lose.

"I am so very sorry," Gael whispered. He'd meant to ask how Jake was feeling, but those words came out instead.

Jake's shoulders lifted slightly as he inhaled and moved away from Gael. "I understand," he mumbled as he sat up gingerly. He put a hand out to the nightstand and stood slowly.

"Can I—"

"No." Jake stumbled to the bathroom and closed the door.

Gael sat immobile. He heard the sound of the toilet flushing after a minute, and then the water from the tap. The bathroom door opened, and Gael winced. Jake's face was awful. Black and purpling bruises tracked up the left side of his neck, jaw, and cheek. Any farther and it would have given him a black eye. Jake walked to the bed and drained the glass of water that sat there. Gael glanced at his phone. It was six.

Gael swung his legs out of bed. "How are you feeling?"

Jake put the glass down. "Headache's manageable. Face is sore, but I've had worse," he said quietly and sat on the bed, his back to Gael as if he didn't want to look at him.

Gael didn't blame him.

He picked up the jeans he had worn yesterday. "Give me ten minutes and I'll be out of your hair," Gael said. He watched as Jake's shoulders dipped.

"If you want."

Gael stopped as he was just about to put a foot into his jeans and stared at Jake's back. *If you want.* Was Jake really giving him a choice, or was Gael hearing things he wanted to, not what was actually being said?

"I didn't mean to keep it from you," Jake whispered, his voice cracking as if every word had sharp edges. "Gregory shocked the fuck out of me when he partnered us. But then…." Jake hesitated.

"Shit happened," Gael said, putting his jeans back down on the floor. He walked around the bed and stopped. He so wanted to sit. Jake seemed to gulp a breath and dropped his head so it was resting in his hand, his eyes covered.

"Sawyer was right. We didn't check, but that's what SWAT is. We have to make split-second decisions. I wish it was different—had been different. I got transferred to ENu pretty easily and the opening was here, but I wouldn't have cared where it was. My experience in SWAT was exactly what they were looking for, but I didn't know what they were like. Then I met your team, and realized I wanted to be on it because that was where I could do the most good."

Gael did sit then, taking comfort in the fact Jake didn't tell him to fuck off, but he barely noticed either. He stopped talking and just sat with his face buried in both hands.

It was ridiculous in a way. They were both suffering. Both seeking forgiveness for a guilt that wasn't their fault. Gael had hurt Jake when he had done his best to try to redeem himself, but really there wasn't anything to forgive, and Gael? He should know better. He was better than this. If fighting to protect Wyatt had taught him anything, it was that his ugly was only skin-deep. He wasn't the best person in the world, but he was no means the worst, and somewhere in the last few weeks, he'd forgotten that. Forgotten himself.

Gael swallowed and raised his hand, then let it hover for a few seconds while he dredged up a little more courage. He let his hand fall on Jake's bare thigh, nearly snatched it back when Jake stilled, but he had to know. Was it guilt? Subconsciously? Or was Jake really attracted to him?

"I have somewhere to go. I'm not homeless and I'm not defenseless. Yeah, life's shit sometimes, but I got carried away with my own pity party. There are a lot of people a ton worse off than me."

Jake let his hands fall and covered one of Gael's, raising his head and looking at Gael. "Room for another at that party of yours?"

Gael smiled, staring at the swelling on Jake's face. "Shit, your face looks awful."

Jake grinned, then clutched his jaw. "Ow, fuck. I can't smile."

Gael leaned forward and kissed the bruising. When he leaned back, he watched as Jake's eyes got stormy. "How about we start again, partner?"

Jake grunted. "There's no way Talon's gonna swap us back. I think we're stuck until Vance's partner shows up."

"Yeah—penance. You got Vance and I got Drew."

Jake pointed to his jaw. "You deserve him."

Gael grinned. "How about you get a shower and I'll go make breakfast?"

Jake's eyebrows lifted. "Or how about you help me shower, seeing as I'm injured?"

Gael smiled slowly and held out his hand. "You may have a point."

JAKE MOANED softly as Gael's firm but gentle hands smoothed soap on his back, up to his neck, and dug in the tight, sore muscles. He felt lips press between his shoulder blades and moaned again. "Not fair," he muttered. "I want a proper kiss."

"I think that's gonna have to wait a few days," Gael replied. "At least until the swelling has gone down. I'm sor—"

"If you apologize again, I'm gonna get mad," Jake spat. "Starting again, remember?"

Gael pressed another kiss to his back in acquiescence.

"Besides, there are other things I can do that don't involve lips... mine, anyway," Jake mumbled, his voice cracking as Gael's hand dug into the curve of his spine and smoothed the ache away over his buttocks. When Gael brought his other hand around to Jake's aching shaft, Jake made a noise that didn't qualify as speech.

"That good?" Gael whispered as he clasped Jake tighter.

Two hands. One pulling his cock and one fondling his balls. Fuck, but he was in heaven.

"Ungh," Jake grunted in appreciation, but Gael must have understood the sentiment because he got a kiss to the small of his back. Gael nuzzled in his neck, dropping kisses, mouthing his skin, and pulling oh so gently with his teeth. Shivers ran down Jake's spine even as a deep, glorious ache started in his groin and his balls tightened. He leaned heavier on the glass, his arm slipping a little, and Gael brought around his arm, anchoring him and drawing him back against his chest.

"I got you," he said, and some switch flicked in Jake and he gave all his weight to Gael, who stood effortlessly, supporting him. The ache rushed through his shaft, and bone-deep pleasure chased it. Jake's lips parting soundlessly, his whole body shaking from the orgasm rippling through him.

He barely remembered Gael getting him dry and into bed. He felt the soft kiss on his forehead and heard the admonishment to take a nap while Gael made breakfast. He didn't remember if he replied. Probably not.

"THAT SMELLS good," Jake murmured sleepily as he inhaled the delicious aroma from the breakfast Gael carried in.

Gael chuckled, put the tray down, deftly stacked some pillows, and helped Jake sit up.

Jake was ridiculously pleased to see two plates, and he dipped his head in alarm as his eyes suddenly burned.

"Hey." Gael lifted his chin, the blue eyes wide and worried.

Jake swallowed, shaking his head, pleading with Gael not to ask. He didn't know why he had suddenly morphed into a sap. Must be the injury. Maybe he really had a concussion and the sudden urge to bawl like a baby was a symptom.

Gael pressed his lips to Jake's forehead, his large hand sliding around to cup his uninjured cheek. "You need to eat, and I happen to know the really good cook who slaved downstairs for an hour will be pissed if you let it get cold."

Jake chuckled as much as he could without smiling widely. It hurt too much.

Gael stepped back and handed Jake two pills. Jake looked at them suspiciously. "I asked Doc Natalie, and she called in a prescription."

"You went out?" Jake looked in surprise at the clock. Wow—he must have slept for a good two hours.

"Well, there was nothing to eat in any of those cupboards down there," Gael said dryly. Gael nudged him again, and Jake opened his mouth obediently for the pills. He swallowed the cool water that Gael passed him and sat up, eagerly looking over at the tray. Scrambled eggs, bacon, breakfast potatoes. "All easy-to-eat stuff." Gael handed him a fork and put the tray on his lap. "I didn't do toast because of the chewing, but we can try something a little more adventurous later."

Jake moaned as he shoveled the first forkful into his mouth because it was just so good and he was starving. "So, you can cook, huh?" he said, swallowing.

Gael grinned.

Jake's breakfast seemed to disappear in seconds, and Gael removed the plate and gave him a large glass of juice and a straw. After draining it completely, Jake shuffled out of bed to the bathroom, peed, and brushed his teeth very carefully so as not to hurt his jaw. He was yawning as he came back into the bedroom to find Gael smoothing down a clean sheet onto the bed. "I swear that shouldn't look as inviting as it does."

Gael smirked. "Doc prescribed you something a little stronger than Tylenol now your head's okay."

Jake sighed. "But I wanted to spend some time with you."

Gael got in bed on his back and lifted his arm in invitation. "I'm here?"

Jake moved quickly because that had been a question and he wanted Gael to know he was welcome. He yawned again. "Ow," he complained as his jaw stretched, although the pain seemed to be subsiding. He got into bed and laid his head on Gael's chest. He loved the steady *thump, thump* in his ear. It grounded him, even if his thoughts were getting a little fuzzy around the edges.

"I hate taking medicine," he murmured, feeling his body relax.

"Yeah, I'm guessing you hate giving up control," Gael said and brushed a kiss into Jake's hair.

"Mmm," Jake responded, more for acknowledging Gael had said something rather than to admit his point. He blinked, realizing his eyes had drifted shut. "Has Talon called?"

"No, but he said he wouldn't unless there was something to say."

Jake's eyes closed again, and it was too hard to push them open. "I was gonna help you move all your stuff."

"Plenty of time for that later."

THE NEXT time Jake woke up, he felt tons better, except he was alone. He could hear faint sounds coming from the other room and guessed Gael was finally unpacking, which was good.

He got out of bed and went to look at himself in the bathroom mirror. The bruises looked darker, but the swelling was down. He opened his mouth experimentally and was happy when he got barely a twinge. His head was clear. He brushed his teeth again and drank the full glass of water—still cold, so he knew Gael had freshened it for him. Jake dragged his cargo shorts on and went in hunt of his nurse. He leaned on the door, watching Gael stuff some papers into a drawer in the nightstand.

Gael looked up and raked his eyes up and down his body. Jake had left his chest bare.

"How are you feeling?"

Jake opened his mouth to reply just as Gael's phone rang.

Gael put it on speaker. "Hey, Talon."

"How's Jake?" came the immediate question.

"A ton better, but you've got to stop Gael from feeding me drugs," Jake chimed in.

They both heard the low chuckle from the phone. "Seriously, Jake. How are you feeling?"

Jake pushed himself away from the door. The question seemed serious. "No trace of headache or blurred vision. My jaw aches when I laugh so I'm cutting that right out."

"Gael?" Talon asked, obviously wanting his opinion.

"Yeah, his head's thicker than I thought."

"Why?" Jake asked, because he didn't think Talon was just casually inquiring.

There was a beat of silence. "Because we've just gotten a call from Mateo Huras. His girlfriend wants to speak to you, and when I suggested you two might not be available, he kind of shut down. I think it's better if you go, as he knows you both from before. But only if you're okay. I can send Finn. Every man and his dog likes him."

Gael laughed, and Jake wondered why Talon sounded defensive. Gael's eyes crinkled assessingly at Jake. "On the condition that if you get any of those symptoms, we cut the visit short," Gael qualified.

It was Talon's turn to laugh. "If it's any consolation, Jake, he's been ordering me around for years." He hung up.

Jake raised his eyebrows. He couldn't imagine anyone having the balls to order Talon around.

"And I drive," Gael said as Jake disappeared into his room to get dressed.

Jake tried not to smile as he hurried to find a shirt. "Do we need to go in uniform?"

"I don't think so. I know Gregory is very strict on that, but technically we're off, and you're injured, even."

Jake winced a little as he pulled the black shirt down over his head. He was going to pick his favorite white one, but he needed something to mute the color palette on his face. He also wasn't going to attempt to run a razor over his bruises.

He glanced up as Gael walked in and smiled in appreciation. Black chinos and a dark gray shirt. Simple, not in any way flashy, but fuck, he looked good. Beautiful guys who dressed with care made Jake immediately want to undress them. Gael had been appearing in hoodies, sweats, and jeans for the past few weeks. Every time he saw him, it was that look or his uniform, but….

"I've suddenly got a real bad ache and think I need to lie down." He'd tried to keep his voice serious, but the accompanying lick of his lips gave it away.

"Your head?" Gael inquired in mock innocence and stepped real close. His hand drifted across the bulge in Jake's jeans.

"No," he whined.

"Later," Gael promised and took his hand to lead him downstairs. It was nice.

AMY NEALSON, Mateo's girlfriend, was nervous, and Jake didn't think the bruises on his face were helping.

Mateo had just whistled when he saw him and asked what the other guy looked like.

Jake didn't dare look at Gael.

They were meeting at Mateo's apartment this time, as it had been released back to them after the forensics people had finished. Toxicology was going to take four weeks, but as Adero's body worked differently from other people's in the water, unless there was evidence he had been sedated, they had nothing to go on.

Amy wrung her hands. "I'd completely forgotten. It was only when we were going through Adero's things that I realized." She paused and looked at Gael. "I remembered your boy in the photograph."

Jake looked excitedly at Gael. "Who is he?"

Amy grimaced prettily. "I'm sorry, I don't know his real name. The other boys called him 'Skin.'"

"Other boys?" Gael asked.

"Why don't you start at the beginning and I'll make coffee?" Mateo suggested, standing.

Amy smiled and took a breath. "I'm a youth group coordinator at Blessed Be on Hillsborough and 59th. We have a popular food-drive program, and we take the older teenagers, with parents' permission, to distribute."

"And they're not afraid of some of the areas they go in. Nebraska Ave, Old Port Tampa, etcetera," Mateo said and went to the kitchen.

Jake looked at Gael for clarification. "Nebraska?"

"Some areas of it are popular with working girls," Gael explained.

"And boys," Amy added. "The photograph you showed me was old—very old, which is why I didn't recognize him at first. I'm guessing he's about seventeen, eighteen now."

Jake didn't correct her use of the present tense.

"And you met Skin on Nebraska?"

Amy shook her head. "No, this was on Kissimmee Ave, Old Port Tampa. There was a bar down there that the prostitutes would go to. I think it's been demolished recently for new housing."

"Did Adero know him?" Gael asked.

"I don't think so. Adero wasn't a member of my church."

"Do you know why he was called Skin?" Jake thought it odd for a name for a prostitute.

Amy nodded, her eyes growing a little misty. "He had a reputation for being hard-core. You know a lot of them won't allow marks of any sort? Apart from the hurt, other clients like the ones with the smooth skin, baby faces."

Jake sighed. He had come across that a lot when he was a beat cop. Johns often liked the younger-looking ones.

"You know he was enhanced?" she asked.

"Yes," Gael replied, but they hadn't, not really. "Do you know what abilities he had?"

"It was common knowledge. Skin would let his clients do anything to him—cut, bruise, bite, you name it—so long as he could walk away and they paid him a ton of money, he was good."

Gael frowned. "So... he didn't feel pain?"

"Oh, yes, he felt pain," Amy insisted, and Mateo came back with the coffees. He sat next to Amy and put an arm around her. "The thing was, whatever they did to him, so long as he ate, his skin would be completely healed in around three hours."

"What?" Jake was incredulous. He looked at Gael. "Have you ever heard anything like that?"

But Gael wasn't looking at him. All his focus was on Amy.

"What do you mean, so long as he ate?"

"He had to eat to repair his skin. I have never seen someone so slim with such an appetite. Seriously, I bet diet companies would have paid him a ton of money to be able to research what made him like that."

Oh, shit. Jake had been slow, but Gael had picked up on it straightaway.

"And if he didn't eat, what would happen?" Gael clarified.

"He'd be in a lot of pain for a much longer time," Amy said bluntly. "His injuries would heal at the same rate as everyone else."

And the man in the storeroom had been starved.

Jake felt almost sick. This wasn't an accident. This wasn't someone being forgotten, or his tormentor prevented from coming back. This was deliberate, and Jake would bet with everything in him that his killer knew about his ability and had used it to torture him.

Jake stood, unable to keep still.

Adero Huras. He had died because he hadn't been able to get in the water to use his ability, and he had *drowned* while he was in bed.

Jake stared in shock at Gael, and Gael stared back with sick understanding in his eyes. Gael had worked it out as well. Whoever was doing this wasn't just targeting enhanced. He was using their own abilities to torture and, eventually, murder them.

Chapter Thirteen

"I'M CALLING Talon. I think we need to bring Cortes and Ryker in on this as well," Gael said as they walked back to the truck.

Jake put his hand on Gael's shoulder, and Gael turned sad eyes to his. "This is what I'm thinking it is, right?"

"That some sicko isn't just targeting enhanced, but he's using their ability to kill them," Gael said, his voice dry, brittle, and it wasn't a question; it was a confirmation.

"That is sick, I agree," Jake said, getting in the car, "but it's also very, very clever." This wasn't some random hate crime. This had taken a lot of thought.

They drove to the office mostly in silence. Jake called Talon, who listened quietly, didn't offer an opinion, just said he would call the others and see them both soon. Then he called Detective Ryker. She was intrigued and promised to meet them as soon as she could get there.

They both walked into the office, and Drew came out of the locker room. "I was here already and just got Talon's call."

Didn't this guy have a life? But then to be fair, if Drew was hoping to join the BAU, he had to be single-minded about his career.

Jake and Gael got coffee ready for everyone as the guys started arriving. Jake watched quietly as the team interacted. They were close. It was interesting how they all treated Finn like he was their little brother. In fact, most of them called him "kid," and at twenty-four, that must have been annoying, but he just took it happily. Sawyer came in, and Jake was surprised to see Eli with him. Jake hadn't had much to do with him. Eli's stature was interesting. All the enhanced Jake had seen were tall and quite bulky, but Eli was slim and not much different in height from Finn. The only similarity was his obvious scar.

Jake stood deliberately, and Sawyer turned defensively, obviously remembering his last words yesterday.

Jake put a hand out to Eli. "We haven't really met, but I'm Jake." He'd seen Eli when he reported on the child he was helping, but between that and the different training they'd all been on, they had barely been in the same room twice.

Eli's eyes widened as he stared at Jake's face, and then his gaze dropped to Jake's outstretched hand. Jake didn't say anything else, just waited. After a few seconds, Eli shook his hand so briefly if he'd blinked, he would have missed it. He didn't say a word, but Jake counted it as a win.

Cortes arrived a minute later, followed by Ryker.

"Gregory is in Orlando and can't make it, but I will keep him up to date," Talon started. He looked at Gael. "Want to explain why we're here?"

Gael quickly explained what Amy Nealson had told them.

"Are you saying that the vics were deliberately targeted?" Cortes asked as soon as Gael paused.

"Not necessarily," Jake answered while Gael took a slurp of his coffee. "The opportunity may have had to present itself, but whoever is doing this has to have an understanding of enhanced."

"Individually or collectively?" Ryker asked.

"Both," Vance said. "Collectively, because he can't be scared. I mean, most people see an enhanced walking down the street, they cross it."

"And individually because they would need to know how to kill them," Cortes answered his own question.

"It could still be a coincidence," Gael carried on. "Adero in particular."

"No toxicology, yet?" Ryker asked.

Cortes shook his head.

"Why not Skin? A coincidence, that is," Sawyer asked.

"Because his ability was well-known. Everyone knew the only way he could recover quickly was by eating."

"That's some scary metabolism," Ryker mused.

"Let's start at the beginning," Talon said.

"We think the murders were all connected because of the photographs," Vance said.

"Then we have to discount Maria Kelly," Drew pointed out. "She was neither enhanced, nor was there a photograph left."

"Unless—" Crap, Jake was so damn slow. "Unless Maria was killed first. The killer did it to get to Derrick, used electricity because of his ability, but he was at a traffic light. He quite possibly *ran out of time*."

Ryker narrowed her eyes. "That's a lot of ifs, Agent."

"The tablet," Gael said slowly. He glanced at Eli. "You're able to help Bo because you can channel another ability linked to your own. You create fire, but Bo couldn't burn you." He looked around, excitement on his face. "What if the murderer did try to electrocute Derrick, but it didn't work? All he succeeded in doing was destroying the computer because Derrick was holding it at the time, so the energy went through him unharmed but wrecked his tablet?"

Everyone was silent, various degrees of comprehension and surprise showing on their faces.

Cortes opened his file. "Maybe we should go right back to the beginning. What information do we have on Dale Smith?"

"He was one of the foster children from the home who disappeared originally. We thought he was taken by Nolan Dakota, but he has always denied all knowledge. I understand from the decomposition of the body, he was dead before Alan Swann started taking the enhanced," Talon said.

"So, the murderer started doing this before all this with the foster kids had even started?" Sawyer asked. "And the two things might not be connected at all?"

"What's next, then?" Gael asked.

"You need to go see Derrick," Talon replied.

A flash of irritation passed over Ryker's face. "We haven't gotten permission to do so yet."

"Gael is the only one who has managed to get him to communicate at all," Jake pointed out defensively.

"Which could lead to the assumption that Agent Peterson is by no means unbiased in this," she said flatly, and Gael squeezed Jake's leg in warning to keep quiet. She sighed. "I'm not wanting to be difficult, but any prosecutor worth his salt could make an argument for that."

Cortes stood and extended his hand to Gael, then nodded to Jake. "Thank you for keeping us in the loop."

Everyone stood and the meeting broke up. The detectives left.

"There's something else," Finn said, and all the team turned to look at him.

"Something you didn't want to say with those two here?" Jake asked, but he pretty much guessed it when Finn went slightly pink in the cheeks.

"When Swann held me—" He hesitated. "—he'd just captured you and Sawyer." Finn nodded at Talon. "I put it in my report, but we never found out how he knew about Talon's increased abilities. I got the distinct impression someone was feeding him information, confidential information. There were a lot of people there when you disintegrated Manning's earrings, so we guessed someone there could have told her."

"Like ENu," Sawyer said pointedly.

Jake tried not to roll his eyes.

"I just think it's something we need to remember," Finn said. "It's someone comfortable with enhanced."

"The badge," Jake reminded everyone. "We still think it's likely it was a cop, or someone dressed as a cop, that got Maria to lower her window."

"We need to go through the addresses that Amy Nealson sent us," Gael reminded Talon.

"I don't mind doing that," Drew volunteered. "I feel like I haven't exactly been pulling my weight around here, and I was going to hang around and do some research anyway."

"Okay, we'll meet back tomorrow. I'll call Gregory and bring him up to speed." Talon turned and eyed Jake. "Go home." He looked at Gael. "Chain him to the bed to keep him there if you have to."

Jake tried really, really hard not to look happy about it.

GAEL LOOKED across at Jake again when they paused at the light. His color was shit, and he didn't mean the black-and-blue bruising; he meant the rest of his face. "How do you feel?"

Jake rolled his head to look at him. "I need a nap," he said with a little self-depreciating humor thrown in.

"Headache, nausea, blurred vision?"

"No, Mom," Jake drawled and closed his eyes. "Well, headache, yeah," he admitted. "I just want to sleep, and then I'm wondering if you could get that amazing cook who's just moved into my place to make some dinner."

Gael smiled and turned the corner as steadily as he could so as not to jostle him.

"You know," Jake continued with his eyes still closed, "I don't suppose any of Vance's brothers work vice, do they?"

"No." Gael shook his head. "Why?"

"Because it would be good to get another insight into Skin's ability. Name, etcetera. I know Cortes is looking, but we know sometimes talking to someone they're comfortable with helps. I haven't been here long enough to develop any connections yet."

"Connections? You mean, cops?" Gael was interested. He tended to forget Jake had been a cop before he had started with SWAT.

Jake smiled lazily but kept his eyes closed. "Yeah, but only to get introductions."

Gael frowned even though Jake couldn't see him. "You lost me."

Jake turned his head again and opened both eyes. "I mean, the cops who work in those areas should all have contacts among the girls. If we're real lucky, they would have them among the boys as well. Asking his peers what he's like is going to get you more info a lot faster. I would imagine that's what Cortes is doing, only he's not enhanced so he might not be asking the right questions."

Gael turned onto 9th and suddenly had a flash of green eyes and blue hair. His smile was wide.

"What?"

He turned, not realizing he was being watched. Jake was listening and had noticed the smile. "I know a rent boy."

Jake didn't move. His eyebrows didn't rise, nor did his breathing alter, but Gael knew he had every drop of the man's attention.

"I don't mean that," Gael replied to the unspoken question, and he pulled up by the pink house. He got out and came around to Jake's side, even though Jake had already gotten out and was shielding his eyes from the sun. Shit, Jake should have worn sunglasses. "And I don't have any you could borrow."

Jake blinked. "Huh?" He stepped up to unlock the door.

"I don't wear sunglasses," Gael said quietly, shyly.

Jake pushed the door open and toed off his sneakers. "Don't like them?"

"No, I mean, I don't need them. Ever since my skin changed, if the sun's too bright, my eyes seem to shade themselves." It sounded ridiculous, and to be honest, he hadn't really questioned it. Along with everything else, it seemed minor. In fact, come to think about it, the doc had asked him if he ever had any vision changes and he'd said no because everything still looked the same, just not as glaring.

Jake stopped and stared, and Gael nearly broke out in a sweat, looking at his dumbfounded expression. What if it was one weird thing too many?

"That is unbelievably cool," Jake said in an awed voice. "Do you know how much money I literally throw away by dropping mine and scratching them, or throwing them on the seat when I get out of the truck and squashing them 'cause I'm too dumb to look when I get back in?"

Gael grinned. Jake was funny, and somehow he still seemed to like Gael, weirdness and all. Jake turned around and trudged up the stairs. Gael went to the fridge and pulled out a bottle of water, then followed him.

In barely a few seconds, Jake was already down to his briefs and pulling back the sheet. He groaned loudly as he lay down. Gael picked up the bottle of pills and shook two out. Jake whined in protest.

"On a scale of one to ten, how much is your face hurting?"

"Five," Jake muttered.

Gael arched an eyebrow.

"Okay, maybe seven," Jake grumbled. He obediently swallowed the pills and took a long drag of the water. Gael watched the swallow trail the length of Jake's throat and cleared his throat. Why should that of all things be unbelievably hot? Jake eased himself down and his eyes fluttered shut. "So tell me about rent boys," he cajoled.

Gael sat on the edge of the bed and absently smoothed the sheet over Jake's side. "You've seen me. You know what I look like, and you know how frightened people are."

Jake reached out and caught Gael's hand, which was tucking the sheet over his arms. He opened his eyes. "I know, and that doesn't have anything to do with me, *with us*. I kind of slept my way across the country coming here. That's why I wanted you to know I was clean, and there hasn't been anyone since my last test, but we should take another first, just to be safe. I've never gone bareback, ever." He took a breath. "I've never wanted to before."

Gael's heart missed a beat. Before? *Before him?* "Yes... I mean, me too. I mean, no, not ever, but maybe yes now." He wanted to die. Since when did he—of every fucking guy on the planet—lose the ability to communicate with any semblance of coherency?

Jake's smile was wicked but not mocking. He locked eyes with Gael and slowly brought Gael's hand up, turned it over, and kissed his palm.

Gael decided that his immediate problem wasn't speaking—it was pulling air into his lungs.

"Now that we've established which rent boys I don't mean, how about we talk about the ones I do?"

He was going to look pathetic. *No.* He sighed. He was going to look even *more* pathetic. "I finally got up the courage to go for a drink in Ybor. I normally hate packed bars like the Westgate, but I thought it might be quiet early on."

Jake scowled. "Yeah, Bernie's cool, but some of the customers are douches."

"Oh," Gael said. "You like it?"

"I like the pool table and the quiet during the day," Jake replied.

Gael focused on Jake's fingers. He hadn't let go of his hand, and his thumb was drawing steady circles on it. "Well, Mac and Carter came in. I was just leaving anyway." He wasn't going to admit to being chased out, but Jake's hand tightened a little on his. "I went outside and ran right into a huge group of partygoers." He waved at his face, knowing that would save him an explanation. "I ducked into the alley that runs alongside it and got propositioned." Gael smiled at the memory but realized Jake's fingers had stopped and looked at his face. Jake's eyes had narrowed, glittering, and Gael immediately wanted to soothe him. "What I mean is, before I told him I *wasn't interested*, he was kind of mouthy, not a bit scared. He asked me if I was a cop."

"He did?" Jake relaxed, then covered his mouth to stifle a yawn.

Gael smiled. "Close your eyes." He couldn't resist smoothing his fingers down the unhurt side of Jake's jaw. Jake hummed a little as if he liked it. "It's just, I think he would make a good contact. He already thinks I'm a cop and he wasn't fazed. Maybe I should take a quick run down there and see if there was any sign of him?"

"Not on your own." Both of Jake's eyes shot open and fixed on his.

Gael hadn't realized he'd spoken out loud. But instead of being offended at the order, he was touched. "I won't go unless Vance can come."

Jake smiled faintly and sighed. His eyes were closing again. "Damn drugs," he muttered,

Gael leaned down and brushed the barest kiss over Jake's lips. He went to lean back, but the groan and the chase of lips from Jake was too much to resist. A rush of heat raced through Gael's body. He pulled away and dropped a kiss on Jake's nose. Jake scowled and he chuckled.

"If I go now, how about I come back, make us some dinner, and we enjoy a lazy evening in bed?"

Jake murmured his agreement, but this time he didn't even manage to open his eyes.

Gael stood for a second and just stared. He didn't believe in God, but just in case anyone was listening, he sent a quick hope heavenward for him not to screw this up. Jake was gorgeous and he wanted to keep him. He breathed out. He wanted Jake to want to keep *him*.

"WHAT?" GAEL said defensively as Vance got in his truck and shot him a look.

"Tell me again what we're doing?"

Gael grinned. "We're going to see if we can find a twink with blue hair and freckles."

"And your boyfriend's not gonna mind?"

Gael opened his mouth to protest and then closed it. *Boyfriend?* Vance's smile got wider when Gael didn't answer. "Shut up," Gael groused and headed for Ybor, which, even though he had had to collect Vance, didn't seem to take long. He pulled up not too far from the center.

Vance got out and looked at his watch. "Isn't it a little early?"

"I read online, this guy who was taking his nine-year-old to school got blocked in by another car. When he got out to ask him to move, there was a pro inside sucking some guy off. It was seven in the morning," Gael added dryly.

Vance grunted but didn't sound surprised.

Gael looked up at him. "The trouble is, I have no idea whether this guy normally hangs out around here or whether he was on his way somewhere."

Vance grunted again. "Well, why don't you ask him?"

Gael was about to shoot off a sarcastic retort when he realized Vance wasn't looking at him. He whipped his head around to where Vance was staring, and nearly dropped in shock. Mr. Blue Hair was leaning up against the cigar shop's front window right across the street.

Before Gael could move or say anything, the twink noticed them and his face lit up. In a flash, he was jogging across the road to where they were both rooted to the spot. Gael looked up at Vance, wondering why the sarcastic comments weren't coming, but Vance stood openmouthed, staring at the sparkly vision that came to a dramatic stop in front of them both.

"Hi, guys," he greeted breathlessly like he had just run a half marathon instead of twenty feet.

Gael grinned. He couldn't help it. "I was hoping to see you."

Blue Hair arched an eyebrow. "I don't do BOGOs."

Vance spluttered, and Gael cracked up even more. "*BOGO?*"

The dimples came out. "Blow one, get one."

Vance snorted rather loudly, and Blue Hair eyed him up and down, his voice suddenly becoming deep and sultry.

"Although, maybe I could make an exception." He shuddered. "Big guys really get me going."

Vance's smile fell, and he went bright pink.

The little guy ran a blue nail across Vance's chest "You big all over, huh?"

Gael watched in complete fascination as the pink in Vance's face turned to a deep red, and his gaze dropped as his feet shuffled.

"But failing that...." He seemed to take pity on Vance and turned to Gael. "What can I do for you, hotshot?"

Gael grinned. It was strange, but somehow he wasn't at all nervous this time. Maybe it was the thought of having his own hotshot waiting back at home that settled him. He had a confidence that usually only came with the uniform.

"I need to ask you a question," Gael said solemnly.

"What's your name?" Vance asked before Gael got the chance to say any more.

Gael glanced at Vance in surprise.

His green eyes twinkling, he held out a hand to Vance. "Angel."

"Angel," Vance repeated, taking his hand gingerly, seeming completely starstruck.

Gael coughed loudly, and Vance dropped Angel's hand as if it had burned him.

Angel looked to the side, twirled around, and ducked into the gap where the trash cans were. After a second, Gael and Vance followed. "So, what do you want to know?" Angel asked.

"You wanna see a badge?" Gael asked.

"Don't need to." Angel smirked. "Just for God's sake, don't ever go undercover like they do on TV." He eyed Vance. "That one's got cop written all over him."

Vance puffed out his huge chest a little more, like Angel had given him a huge compliment, but Gael frowned. "Enhanced aren't allowed to be cops."

Angel sighed and inspected a blue nail. "You got two minutes."

Gael quickly asked him if he'd seen any enhanced turning tricks and described Skin.

"Where was his patch?" Angel asked, and Gael told him. Angel cocked his head on one side. "You're talking about Simon, aren't you?" Gael started to shrug. "Skin," Angel added quietly.

"Yes," Vance said.

"I've heard of him. I've never met him, but the Old Port was cleared out before I moved up here." Angel bit his lip. "You got a card?"

Vance beat Gael to the one in his pocket.

Angel stared at the card Talon had made for them all, and smiled. "Give me a day, Agent," he said, pocketing it. Gael had no idea how he even fit paper in those skintight jeans. He blew them both a kiss but winked at Vance, turned on a delicate heel, and was gone.

"Wow," Vance said in amazement.

Gael eyed Vance, not knowing what to say. "You okay?"

"I'm in love," Vance pronounced in all seriousness.

Gael laughed shortly, not 100 percent convinced Vance was joking. "Come on. I wanna go home." He had to drag Vance, though.

Chapter Fourteen

JAKE NEVER stirred when Gael shucked off all his clothes, ready to slide under the covers. He was lying on his side with his bruised side faceup. Gael felt a pang of remorse and then took a breath. Enough. They'd both had enough of that.

Gael padded around to the other side of the bed and slowly got in. He slid closer to Jake and spooned him.

"I have a gun."

Gael sniggered. "On you?"

Jake chuckled, rolled onto his back, and lifted an arm. "C'mere."

Gael obeyed instantly.

"What time is it?" Jake squinted at his clock.

"Nearly nine. I had to take Vance home."

"So what happened tonight?"

"Well, Vance fell in love." Gael grinned and told Jake all about Angel. "He's gonna call us tomorrow."

"You think he will?"

Gael paused, thinking about the way he'd been pleased to see them, how he hadn't been a bit scared. "Yeah, I think so."

Gael kissed the patch of skin he was lying on. Jake had quite a few black chest hairs smattered around each nipple, and suddenly Gael's mouth watered. Without stopping or questioning the impulse, he lifted his head and sucked a nipple right into his mouth.

"Fuck," Jake gasped and nearly lifted off the bed.

Gael let go with a pop. "Don't like?"

"You kidding me?" Jake returned weakly, so Gael bent his head again.

This time Jake stayed where he was, but the accompanying moan was very good. Gael licked and laved the hard bud while his fingers strayed to the other to tease and scrape with his nail. He let go and started kissing and sucking down Jake's chest and abdomen.

Jake suddenly tightened his fingers in Gael's hair, where he had been hanging on. "No, please," he husked. Gael raised his eyes and stared into Jake's. Dark midnight pools begged back at him. He dropped a kiss on Jake's lips and turned over on his stomach.

"How long?" Jake whispered, coming up on one elbow, trailing two fingers down Gael's spine, and he shivered into the touch.

Gael swallowed. "Years," he admitted.

Jake kissed the small of his back. "Then we're gonna go real slow," he promised. Gael tried to get comfy, but he was already semihard. Jake sat up and reached over to the nightstand. He fished around in the drawer and took out a small square packet and a tube. "Get up on your knees, baby. I don't want to hurt you."

Gael did, but he knew his cheeks were reddening a little.

"Hush," Jake comforted as if he knew. His hands smoothed over Gael's ass, and he seemed in no hurry to reach for the lube. Jake shuffled until he was behind him, and he bent to trail kisses all the way down Gael's spine.

Gael swallowed. The kisses were gorgeous, but he was nervous. Despite him wanting this, the two times he had done this had hurt like hell. The second time he had bled and promised himself never again.

"Hey, sweetheart," Jake said in a low voice. "We can stop, do something different. You just say the word, okay?"

Sweetheart. Gael was a sap, but the word made him melt, and he felt a little tension drain out of his shoulders.

Jake ran his fingers up and down his spine and followed his fingers with his lips. Then he carefully parted Gael's asscheeks and kissed the top of his crease.

"Jake," Gael whispered. Then his eyes widened as he felt the first swipe of Jake's tongue. *Jesus.* "Incredible," Gael sighed, completely unable to contain the word.

Jake squeezed in response, and his tongue dipped lower. Gael moaned. The lower Jake's tongue got, the more noises spilled from Gael's lips, and when Jake skimmed his tongue around Gael's hole, he thought he would die. Or explode. Or pass out from just how good it was.

Jake grunted in response, and then Gael realized he'd been wrong. The moment Jake curled his tongue and pushed it inside was the moment he seriously doubted he would ever need oxygen again.

"Baby," Gael moaned as Jake took his mouth away. Gael heard the click of the tube open, and in another few seconds, Jake's hands were back, slicking his hole with lube. He pushed against Jake's hand, wanting more.

Jake swirled his finger around Gael's hole and dipped the tip in, teasing him; all the while Jake murmured encouraging noises. Jake slid one finger in past the knuckle, and Gael moaned deliriously, begging with his body, begging with his heart. He rocked back in a steady rhythm. Jake added another finger, stretching, rubbing, then more lube. Jake brought his hand around and rubbed his palm over Gael's cock. He didn't need any lube there, as his skin, slick with precum, slid right over. Gael shuddered. It was almost too much, and he bit his lip as a tide of need seemed to swell inside him.

"Jake, please. I wanna feel you and I'm not gonna last."

"We have all night," Jake soothed, but his voice cracked, betraying how close his own need was.

"Please," Gael whispered.

Jake kissed Gael's back and slid his fingers gently out. "I wanted to touch your gland, but I reckoned you'd shoot."

Gael moaned in reply.

"Sweetheart? Promise me if this hurts…."

"Jake!" Gael nearly bellowed in frustration, and he heard a low chuckle from behind him. The condom packet ripped, and seconds later Gael felt Jake's firm fingers and more lube, then pressure as Jake pressed himself against Gael.

"Push out, baby," Jake gasped, and suddenly he was partway in. Jake held himself still, and Gael's eyes

smarted at the burn. He hadn't thought it would actually hurt. He took a few choppy inhales, disappointmen
coursing through him. He had wanted this so much, had
convinced himself it would be different. "Hey," Jake
said gently. "Breathe, baby." Jake withdrew a little, and
Gael relaxed slightly. He felt Jake's cool fingers around
the tightly stretched skin. More lube. Gael took another, deeper breath. Jake pushed back in again, and Gael's
eyes stung. He opened his mouth to say he couldn't. He
was useless. A failure.

Then Jake changed his angle and slid inside some
more. *Fuuuck.* He panted. Jake's hand came around to
fondle his dick, and it sprung up again, rock hard. Jake
did it again, and sparks rushed through Gael and he
moved. "Ohh," he breathed out and clutched the sheet
he was lying on.

"That good, baby?" Jake panted the question as he
slid in and out in time to the pounding in Gael's ears
He couldn't speak. Jake was everywhere at once, in his
body, in his mind. He was whispering in his ear, his large
hands pulling and smoothing his cock until it he could
hardly bear it. Everything throbbed, his skin was alive,
and with every thrust, he was pushed closer and closer to
something so unbelievably good, he wanted to cry.

Just one more. Just one more, and Jake twisted
his wrist and Gael's orgasm thundered through him so
fast and so hard, he could hardly breathe. He knew he
cried out something, and heard the echo behind him as
his body seemed to splinter into a million tiny pieces.
Then he felt the lips pressing to his back, putting every
bit together again.

He realized the noise was him trying to inhale
what little oxygen there was left in the room, and he

felt a tiny burn as Jake slid out, then emptiness. He was suddenly ridiculously glad for the large body that pulled him onto his side so he wasn't lying in his own wet patch.

"Stay there," Jake rumbled behind him, and he got out of bed. In barely a minute, he was back with a warm cloth and tenderly cleaned Gael up.

Gael blinked furiously and struggled to say anything, but when Jake slid back under the covers and pulled him close, it wasn't really necessary.

GAEL GROANED as he rolled over, barely awake. He heard the shower running and stared, bemused, as Jake walked back into the bedroom.

He bent down to kiss Gael. "I'm sorry. I wish I could put you in the bath. A soak would do you good." He swallowed and looked nervous as he waited for Gael to reply.

Gael let his smile spread across his face, and Jake's eyes glittered as he shared the humor, and the memory. Gael stretched cautiously, trying not to wince. "You may have to carry me to the shower."

Jake rolled his eyes. "Get your sore ass in there so I can change the sheets. We're meeting everyone at Betty's at eight."

Gael immediately brightened and he forced himself out of bed.

TWO HOURS later, as Jake and Gael walked into the field office, Jake stared as Finn flew across the room and practically tackled the young enhanced man talking to Gregory.

"Adam!" Finn shrieked, and Adam turned and caught him in a bear hug. They were both laughing and the others all crowded around, slapping Adam's back, shaking his hand.

Gregory just stood back and looked very pleased with himself.

As soon as Finn had shrieked Adam's name, Jake remembered him from reading up on the reports when he had started. Adam had been Finn's childhood best friend until he had transformed at eleven and his parents had moved the entire family away, unable to cope with the shame.

He had been in and out of foster care, run away, lived on the streets, and eventually fallen in with a gang committing bank robberies. Adam could manipulate metal and locks, but his second ability involved electricity. As Jake understood it, though, he was currently in prison for his part in two bank robberies, and despite the fact he saved Finn's life and helped the feds by giving evidence. Gael had no idea how Gregory had gotten him here.

"Sit down, everyone," Gregory said. He looked at Jake. "Adam is out on strict license. Assistant Director Manning has agreed to him helping our unit temporarily, as we have no one with the ability to manipulate electricity, and with the death of Maria Kelly, she has been able to successfully persuade the state's attorney that he should be here rather than in a cell."

Finn glanced at Adam, worry stark on his face.

"If I behave and make myself useful, the gig will be extended," he assured Finn. "That's what the boss lady said anyway."

"And properly addressing her as Assistant Director Manning or ma'am might be a good start," Gregory said dryly.

"Yes, sir," Adam replied promptly, and everyone grinned. Adam grinned back, and then his gaze fell on Jake.

"This is my partner, Jake Riley," Vance introduced him, despite Jake sitting close to Gael and Vance being on the other side of the table.

Jake held out his hand and smiled, trying not to wince. "Good to meet you. I don't normally look this pretty," he quipped.

Adam chuckled, and Jake took him in. Big, like all enhanced, but slim like Eli. He must have had a good four inches in height on Eli, though. Blond hair, but much darker than Gael's, and his eyes were a green-blue color. In fact, if a certain other person wasn't getting all of his attention, Adam would have.

"You can stay with us," Finn pronounced.

Adam shot a surprised look at Talon, and Talon smiled slowly, nodding his agreement. Adam tilted his head and shrugged. "I can't." He pushed himself away from the table and lifted his leg, pulling his jeans up. The thick ankle bracelet was very visible.

All eyes shot to Gregory.

"One of the conditions is that Adam lives at Benchmark House. It's a halfway house for parolees, with strict rules. He has to report there daily, and curfew is ten. He can't leave the state. Random drug testing, not entering any establishment that sells alcohol—"

"What about not associating with criminals, because that's gonna be hard?" Finn asked quickly.

"Provided he is accompanied at all times by one of the team, he is covered for that."

Finn looked distressed.

"Hey, buddy," Adam said. "I'm out." He put his hands out, like *don't forget that's the important thing.*

Finn smiled, but he leaned a little closer to Talon

Jake sighed. He didn't know how he had missed it when he first started. Maybe it took being in love to recognize it in others.

Shit.

Jake breathed through his nose, slowly trying to process what he had just thought. *Love?* He looked at Gael, who must have felt his gaze because he turned and focused those gorgeous blue eyes on him. Jake could feel his cock stirring just because Gael was staring back. He wasn't sure about love, but lust was certainly an L-word he would use around Gael.

He rubbed his chin absently, hating the fact that he hadn't shaved, and hissed slightly because he'd forgotten it hurt to touch it. He was regretting not taking any Tylenol before they left. He'd seen Talon watching him a few times in the diner as he had tried to chew his food without it hurting.

"I'm going to partner Adam up with Eli."

Jake's focus was dragged sharply back to the present, as there was a kind of awed silence following Gregory's words. To be fair, no one looked more shocked than Eli.

"Sir?" Drew cleared his throat. "With respect, and if Gael wouldn't mind, it might be helpful if I partnered Adam."

Talon swung his gaze to Drew. "Why?"

Drew took a hurried breath. "Well, I just thought a human partner might look a little better with the assistant director."

Jake winced at the double insult.

"We're all human, Drew, last time I looked," Talon returned mildly.

"And as trustworthy," Eli said, which was another surprise.

Drew shuffled. "I didn't mean—"

"The assistant director is happy leaving the partnership decisions of the team up to Talon and I," Gregory said with a little more bite than usual.

Drew dropped his gaze to the floor, and Jake felt a little sorry for him. He didn't fit. He didn't fit with the team, and it wasn't because he was a regular; it was because he was a jerk. It was as if Drew felt he had something to prove all the damn time, or maybe Jake wasn't being fair. The rest of the testosterone in this room took a lot of living up to, and apart from Gregory, Drew was the only guy to see the inside of Quantico. Not even Jake had, but Gregory had explained that when he first applied. They might be an offshoot of the FBI, but they were more a specialized consultancy service, and none of them would work on "regular" cases, which suited Jake fine. He had his hands full with exactly what they were doing.

Maybe Drew felt he had a lot to prove? He'd done the training and worked as an agent for three years. Maybe he needed to put out an olive branch, or maybe if Drew got the BAU job he was hoping for, he would never see the guy again.

"So, we're waiting to hear what Angel can come up with," Gregory said, finishing his assessment of the case. "Drew, anything on the addresses?"

"Nothing pertinent as far as I can see, sir."

"What about Derrick?" Gregory asked Gael.

"I'm going back there as soon as I can."

Gael's phone rang just then, and after glancing at it, he excused himself, stepping outside.

Gregory looked at Eli. "Eli, perhaps you would like to take Adam and help him settle in. Benchmark will expect him to check in soon."

Jake watched in fascination as Eli colored slightly but stood, and Adam followed him out just as Gael came back into the room.

"That was Angel. He has information and wants to meet."

Jake went to stand, but then so did Drew. Jake chewed his lip and winced as he pulled his skin.

"Jake," Talon said, the warning in his voice. "I understand your commitment, but enough is enough. You're going home. I didn't object to you coming to the meeting, but fieldwork—"

At that moment all their phones sounded with an alert. Someone wanted the team.

Talon dialed a number, and Jake stared at Gael in frustration. Talon said they would be right there and put his phone back in his pocket. "Fight in a bar, but it looks like an enhanced is involved." He waved Gael and Drew away. "We got this, go." Then he turned to Finn. "Can you please take Jake home?"

"But—" Jake protested as Gael shot him an apologetic look and followed Drew.

"Jake," Talon growled. "When this is done, we'll review the partnerships again, but you are not fit to be at work, and I don't want Gael going anywhere without backup."

Jake subsided and meekly followed Finn out to his car.

ANGEL PICKED up a sweet potato fry and regarded Gael with solemn eyes. "There's another guy,

Ricky. He's worked up here awhile, but he knows Skin from the port. They shared a room down there when they had money, and knew some good places to crash when they didn't. He'll talk to you but no one else." He glanced at Drew. "Sorry."

"You're not meeting on your own, Gael," Drew said stiffly.

Gael arched his eyebrows at the order and ignored Drew. "How long is it since Ricky has seen Simon, did he say?"

"About a month before the room they were squatting in got demolished, ready for the area to be cleared."

"We need to find out an approximate date," Gael mused. "They've been building down there nearly two years."

Angel shrugged. "I've only lived here a few weeks."

"And how reliable is this information?" Drew asked.

Angel rested his gaze on Drew. "Well, I doubt the sort of hotel rooms he visits have bibles in the night-stands, if that's what you mean," he drawled.

"And what else did Ricky tell you?" Gael asked, wishing Drew would be quiet.

"Simon got a new boyfriend," Angel said. "He only saw the back of his head once when he was getting in his car."

"Did—"

"No," Angel answered before Gael could ask. "All he said was that it was a sedan, fancy and a dark blue. Looked new. Money. The guy had brown hair, average build. He was wearing a suit."

Gael lifted a brow. Angel had given them the details without him having to ask. "Was it the first time Simon met him?"

Angel shook his head. "No, the guy had cruised around maybe a week earlier, but he'd kept Simon overnight three times."

"Isn't that unusual in a prostitute?" Drew asked, and Gael cringed.

Angel didn't get annoyed, though. If anything, he seemed to think Drew's holier-than-thou attitude was amusing. "Ricky doesn't know. Simon didn't always say, and he was tight-lipped about this one. Said he had a fancy house."

"He went there?" Drew asked.

"No, but the guy took a call from a lawn-care company, apologizing and saying they were terminating the contract."

Gael stilled. He glanced at Drew, but Drew was still staring at Angel.

"Ricky says he's going to party at Reunion tonight, but he'll give you five minutes before he leaves."

"Where?" Gael asked.

"Wherever his last john drops him off at," Angel said pointedly. "But he always eats in here, so I think if you show up about nine, we shouldn't be far away."

Drew inhaled as if he was going to make another protest.

"If you want to check me out, give Lieutenant Davies from Miami PD over in City Hall a call. He'll vouch for any information I give you," Angel said quietly.

"So, you're a source?" Drew asked.

Angel grinned. "Absolutely. Give him a call." He popped another fry in his mouth and then reluctantly pushed away his half-eaten plate.

"They're not good?" Gael had demolished his.

Angel smirked. "I have to fit in my shorts later." He looked around to make sure no one was listening and leaned forward to Gael. He nodded at Drew. "Not that I don't mind meeting all the fabulous agents you work with, you understand, but I was hoping you were gonna bring the big guy."

Gael nearly choked on his water.

"I'M NOT sure how reliable he is," Drew said as they watched Angel sashay out of the diner.

"What did you mean by a source?" Gael asked.

"Confidential informant."

"That's good, then?"

Drew sighed. "Gael, CIs are only doing it to stop themselves from getting locked up in the first place. Trustworthy isn't a word I'd use around him."

Gael's phone rang again to save him from answering Drew. He frowned at the screen and put it to his ear. "One minute, Michael. Just let me get outside."

Michael sounded frantic. "Gael, Derrick's being accused of attacking another child. They're threatening to transfer him to somewhere secure. Can you get here?"

"On my way," Gael said quickly and looked up to see Drew had followed him outside. "That was Michael Ramsay, the principal from Derrick's school. He got a call five minutes ago from Bayside. Apparently Derrick might have hurt another child and they're threatening to move him to a more secure location. Michael's with him now. I've got permission to go."

Gael fished his keys out, relieved they had traveled in separate cars. "Drew, you need to go and look at those addresses. We both know that was too much of a coincidence. Can you let the team know what's happening?"

Drew looked worried. "I don't like you going on your own."

"They won't let you in if you come. I think having a look and seeing if we can find anything in those addresses is the key. We're missing something, and this might be the connection we need."

"Okay." Drew nodded. "Call me from the hospital as soon as you can, and I'll let everyone know as soon as they get back from the call." He paused. "Are you gonna call Jake?"

Gael shook his head. No, Jake would be frantic and try and come to find him. Jake needed to rest, and there was nothing he could do in the hospital.

Chapter Fifteen

IT TOOK Gael thirty minutes with the traffic to get to Bayside. Michael had sounded worried. Gael had spoken to Gregory, who said child judicial services were involved and basically it was out of their hands. Gael tightened his grip on the steering wheel. Michael hadn't gotten all the details. Something about an argument with another child, but that made absolutely no sense whatsoever.

Michael had been quite definite before. Gael was the only person Derrick had ever communicated with at all. He wasn't capable of having an argument. Even when those boys from the school had wrapped him in the netting and poked him with the sticks, Derrick hadn't fought them. He had cried out until someone had heard him. If he had any enhanced strength, he certainly hadn't used it.

Gael finally pulled into Bayside and looked at his phone just in case he had a text from Jake. Damn, nearly out of battery, and he wasn't allowed to have it in the unit anyway. He opened the glove compartment and shoved it in there in disgust. He would work out how to text Angel later. First he needed to worry about a child who no one else seemed to.

Gael walked quickly to the front desk and was relieved to see Isaac, Derrick's *train* nurse.

"I'm off," Isaac said, "but I told Michael I would wait around for you and buzz you through."

"What happened?" Gael asked as Isaac keyed in the code to let them both through to the ward.

Isaac hesitated and glanced back at Gael. "I don't know, I wasn't there, and I'm not supposed to talk about it with you. I'm sorry."

Gael sighed in frustration and followed Isaac through the door into Derrick's room. Gael blinked. Derrick was curled up in the corner of the bed, shaking. There was a man in a white coat writing something on a chart, and a nurse was drawing up something in a syringe. There were also two security guards in a uniform Gael had never seen before.

"Michael?" Gael said to the principal, who sat on the edge of the bed.

Michael turned and sighed deeply. The nurse picked up the syringe, offering it toward the doctor, and nodded to the guards.

"Wait," Gael asked. "Please, let me talk to him."

The doctor paused. "And you are?"

Gael flashed his ID. "Agent Peterson. I spoke to Derrick briefly yesterday and at the school."

The doctor blinked. "You *spoke* to him?"

Gael nodded. "A mixture of tactile signing and his child's computer." He glanced at the bed, then at Michael. "Where is it?"

The doctor looked nonplussed, but the nurse spoke up. "Barry, one of our other patients, has it. He and Derrick have been sharing it, and we didn't have a problem with that yesterday."

"No, I know that. I mean, the tablet that belongs to Derrick. I had it fixed and brought it in yesterday."

The nurse glanced at Michael. "I didn't know that. The one Barry wanted was the one we have here."

Gael looked at Michael. "What exactly happened?"

The nurse answered for him. "Barry came looking for it even though he shouldn't have been allowed in." She looked pointedly at one of the guards. "I had to leave the room, and Derrick must have wanted to go to the bathroom. He isn't capable of summoning for help and has been going in there himself. I was on my way back when I heard the crying. Barry came running out of the bathroom, insisting Derrick had hit him with the toy. He has quite a bruise."

"Cameras?"

She shook her head. "Not in the bathrooms. We looked at the tape, and it shows Derrick going in there, Barry following him, and then, a minute later, Barry running out crying. Barry has parents and they're not happy."

"They've already contacted a lawyer and are threatening to sue the unit unless something is done," Michael added.

"And you're going to drug him?" Gael was appalled.

"We have permission," the doctor said, a little defensively. "He qualifies under the Enhanced Protection Law."

Gael bit his tongue to stop him from saying anything that might get him thrown out. The Enhanced Protection Law was the same one that gave ENu the powers to forcibly sedate and detain enhanced. It wasn't, as the name suggested, for the protection of enhanced. It was for regular human protection against the enhanced.

The doctor sighed. "I'm sorry, but my hands are tied. At least if we give him something, his dose will be appropriate for his body mass. If we call the ENu, God only knows what they might give him." Which was true.

"And he's frightened." The nurse gestured to Derrick. "We haven't been able to get near enough to make sure he is okay."

Gael sat down carefully on the bed and looked at Michael. "Where?"

Michael swallowed. "He's being transferred to Jackson Memorial."

Gael's mouth dropped open. "No." He looked at Derrick, who was silent, still curled up in a fetal position. Jackson Memorial was a young offender's unit. It was harsh. Gael had seen a documentary arguing for its closure. The boys who were sent there were habitual offenders, and sent there as their last chance. They had interviewed boys who had since been released successfully, and they had described the military precision the place was run with.

It would destroy Derrick. There was no way he could go there.

"He's not going into the young offenders' unit," the doctor said impatiently. "There's a secure adolescent psychiatric unit as a separate wing."

"But he doesn't need it," Gael argued, not liking the sound of that any better. "Derrick has never been violent."